THAT DOESN'T BELONG HERE

Dan Ackerman

Supposed Crimes LLC • Matthews, North Carolina

Published in the United States.

ISBN: 978-1-944591-41-0

www.supposedcrimes.com

This book is typeset in Goudy Old Style.

For David

"Hey, stop," Emily said, smacking Levi with the back of her hand.

Levi paused. "What?"

"Look."

Levi peered over the side of the jetty into the ocean where Emily pointed. "What?"

"*Look*," she insisted.

"Shit, is that a pickup?"

Submerged in the sea was a silver pickup, hard to notice in the early morning light.

They had been out all night, and she had wanted to watch the sunrise before they went home. No one else was on the beach yet. Levi wasn't sure if people were allowed on the beach this early.

"That doesn't belong there," he said. "Weird."

"Fucking beyond weird, man. It's the middle of the ocean. What's it doing here?"

"Maybe it fell off a garbage barge. And I mean, it's not really the middle, the beach is right there."

She gave him a look like he was stupid, which she did a lot, so he barely noticed. He stared down at the truck for a while, trying to think of a reasonable explanation as to why it would be there. Falling off a boat of some kind made the most sense, but boats didn't frequent this beach, especially not ones large enough to carry a pickup.

He didn't notice Emily had pulled off her shorts and t-shirt and tossed them onto the stones of the jetty, not until she had picked her way down the side of the jetty into his line of vision. She was not wearing a bikini top; she insisted that if he didn't have to cover his chest, then neither did she. It was fair; he didn't argue and he tried to pretend it was not distracting. He had stared awkwardly at her face, trying not to look down for most of the summer. He had learned she had freckles over her nose and brown flecks in her blue eyes, sometimes bits of snot dangled from her nose, she didn't always pluck her eyebrows and, when she wore makeup, it caked into the small creases in her skin and clung to the fuzzy, fine hairs on her cheeks.

It was a lot to learn, especially during the summer when he had not planned on learning anything.

"Hey, come on," she said.

He did not peel off his shirt, not wanting her to see what his brother called his 'fatboy tits', his scraggly patch of chest hair or his pasty white skin. He climbed down the jetty.

"Em, I don't know. What if it's dangerous?" He looked at the water uneasily.

She didn't listen and climbed into the water. He followed, hating the way his shirt clung to his skin.

She glanced over at him and said, "You keep swimming with shirts on, you're gonna drownd."

"It's just drown," he corrected.

"Well, then you'll *drown*."

He shook his head. She gave him a look, then took a deep breath and dove underwater. He watched her swim down, her bright orange bikini bottom stark against the ocean's sandy floor, her dark tanned legs kicking and her arms close to her sides.

She swam with her legs, always, because her legs were strong, with thighs that were thick and a little jiggly. Her arms were not, she couldn't do ten push-ups, but she could run for miles.

She popped back up and said, "Levi, get down here," took another breath and disappeared.

He didn't follow, and after a moment, she came back up again. "Seriously, there's something in here."

"Something what?"

"I don't know, something alive."

"Probably a shark, we should get a lifeguard or something. Call the cops."

"Right now," she insisted. She grabbed his hand, not to be argued with.

She hadn't worn makeup today, never wore makeup to the beach, and he could see the dark circles under her eyes, the ones she usually hid with concealer and powder and eyeliner. He'd watched her do it; he'd even let her paint his eyes a few times because she had insisted. When she insisted, he had to obey.

He took a deep breath, filling his broad chest with air. He was solidly built, tall with big hands; his mother told him he could be an athlete if put his mind to it. Emily pulled him underwater, and though the salt water stung his eyes, he could still see through it.

She released his hand and kicked over to the truck, the cab of which was mostly full with water, and pointed to the window of the back seat.

There was something in there, something with a long tail, something curled up on itself. It did not move.

She knocked on the window, but the thing still didn't move. She pointed to a rock on the floor and he knew she wanted him to break the window. It seemed like a bad idea, but he did it, lifting the skull-sized rock and smacking it into the window.

The thing started when he pounded the window, uncurling and then flailing.

With a few blows, the window broke and water gushed in. The thing inside panicked and seemed disoriented, not sure what to do, pushed up against the wall of the truck cab by the rush of water.

Levi, half-pulled by the water, went up against the door and reached his hand out to the thing, hoping to grab it and pull it out.

Whatever it was, it did not belong in the backseat of a pickup truck. He would pull it out, and it would wriggle free, he hoped. He grabbed the first thing he could and pulled it out, but it did not wriggle free, it dangled from his hand like an anchor.

He glanced down to see it had grabbed onto him with something that looked too much like a human hand. It was struggling weakly, pulling him down.

He shook off its grip and hurried to the surface, the edges of his vision starting to go black. Emily was right behind him. He gasped for breath and saw the thing had not surfaced, though it was reaching up for the sky.

Before Emily could tell him to go back down, he went and wrapped his arms around its body and kicked toward the surface.

Once the creature's head broke the surface, it gasped for air, choking and coughing. Levi loosened his grip, and it grabbed on to him again, so he dragged it to the jetty, not without Emily's help.

It flopped wetly against the rocks, breathing hard, wheezing a little.

Emily stared, transfixed. She pointed to the creature's tail, long and whip-like with slender fins around the edges, almost eel, almost dolphin, but not really like either. The tail, pale gray and speckled with black and white, had three deep puncture wounds, as well as a deep gash on one side, not bleeding but still open and irritated, and a half-dozen scrapes and cuts that were fresh, still bleeding, probably from being dragged through the broken window.

On the thing's torso, because it had a torso shaped like a person's—though it was neither distinctly male nor female—were what looked like rope burns.

"Levi," Emily breathed.

"Don't even," he warned.

"It's hurt, though."

The creature had gone still, and she touched it. It looked up at her, its face, which looked too human, just like its hands and arms and torso, pulled tight with unmistakable concern.

She pointed to its tail and asked, "Can you swim?"

It stared at her, then let out a stream of gibberish words accompanied with clicks, hums, and whistles. It made these noises for a while.

She pointed to the ocean, then to its tail and made a swimming motion with her hands.

It hummed and babbled. It wiggled its tail then whined, grimacing.

"I don't think he can swim."

"He?" Levi asked.

"Sure, look at his face. It looks like a he to me," she said.

"What happened to not putting labels on things?"

"That's Charlotte's deal, not mine. I'm fine with labels," she said. "God, she's never going to believe this!"

Charlotte was Emily's long-term but currently long-distance, girlfriend. They had not seen each other since Emily had flown to Iran in the winter; Charlotte would be home at the end of the summer, finishing her last round of classes abroad.

"I wish I had my phone," Emily said.

The creature made a sad, pitiful noise.

"We can't leave him here," she continued. "Someone...I mean, he was in the back of that car...and he's in bad shape." She reached out to touch red marks around his wrists and eyed the corners of his mouth, where the skin raw. "I think someone...well, I think someone had plans for this guy."

Levi couldn't argue because the creature looked more than just tired and beat up, he looked frightened. He couldn't have left a dog behind like this, he certainly couldn't leave whatever this thing was to die on a jetty, to get poked and jabbed by all the tourists who would be here once the sun climbed a little higher in the sky.

"We could bring him to the house," Levi suggested. "The water's nice and calm there."

She nodded. "Yeah, yeah, right."

The creature looked between them, dark eyes flicking back and forth nervously. Emily reached out and put a calm hand on him, rubbing his shoulder.

"You're okay, buddy," she promised.

He seemed a little calmer and even touched her hand. She smiled, and he smiled back, showing sharp teeth.

"I'm gonna go bring the car down, okay, we can get him in. Back in ten." She grabbed her shorts and shirt, pulling them on and sprinting away.

He watched her go, staring for a moment at the way the water soaked her clothes, making them mostly see-through.

It was shitty, he knew, to stare and worse to stare at someone who was taken and didn't even like men, but he was lonely and single since his high school girlfriend had dumped him to go to a different college.

He'd had a few awkward fumblings, one bathroom blowjob and not much else except himself for the past two years.

He was fat (chubby, his mother insisted) and pale, eternally uncomfortable and shy, a far cry from the tanned, lean and confident guys who owned the city and the campus. He looked down at the shirt clinging to him, considering maybe his mother was right, maybe he was just chubby. His doctor had never insisted he lose weight. He had a little bit of a belly, soft and smooth, and his chest was not muscular, it jiggled a little when he walked, but he was not corpulent.

Not yet, he reminded himself, thinking of his father, who'd lost his leg to diabetes and had done little to take care of himself afterward, growing sicker and fatter each year.

His mother was slender and lovely, and she had passed that on to his brother and his two sisters, beautiful, thin people with clear ivory skin and nice smiles.

Only his brother had ever called him fat—his brother and some assholes in high school. Maybe he was just chubby; he wanted to convince himself. Maybe being chubby instead of a weird kid with boy-tits would make it easier to talk to people.

The creature touched his leg, and he jumped, staring down at it. Looking at this lean, slender thing made all of muscle and sinew, he felt fat again, just like he did standing for family pictures.

Emily returned and parked her Jeep at the end of the jetty. She waved at him, called, "Bring him over!" so he slipped back into the water, pulling the creature with him.

The creature balked at being pulled back to the water and fought when he realized he was being brought to shore.

Levi choked on seawater as the creature thrashed, weak but still stronger than Levi had expected. He let go, and the thing slipped underwater, just a hand poking up. Levi took him by his hand and pulled, trying to hurry, hoping the water would disorient him.

By the time he got to the shallows, the creature had recovered, and Emily had rushed down.

"You didn't have to drop him," she scolded.

He didn't answer.

She laid a blanket on the sand and helped him drag creature on to it. The creature continued to fight until she plopped herself onto his chest and sat there for a moment, grabbing his hands and holding them close to herself.

"I'm not trying to hurt you." Her voice came out soft and soothing, the way she talked to stray cats. "You're hurt, you can't stay here. People are coming."

The creature didn't understand, made more of his odd noises, pointing to the sea, trying to pull his hands back.

She didn't let go, and he didn't seem to want to hurt her.

She pointed between herself and Levi and said, "Friends." She touched Levi on the leg and smiled up at him, then said again to the thing, "Friends."

He stared.

She pointed between herself and the creature. "Friends."

He kept staring.

She stood up, pointed to his tail. "You're hurt. Hurt."

He blinked.

"We're going to help, okay. I promise."

He pointed to the ocean but seemed less insistent this time. He looked up at Levi.

Levi didn't know what to say, so he pointed between himself and the creature and said, "Friends. Um..." He made a swimming motion with his hands and pointed to the wounded tail. "No swimming. Hurt." He pointed between himself and Emily. "We'll help you."

He stared, looking scared, but he looked down at his tail, touching the blood that ran down his smooth skin, at the deep wounds. He made a sound they didn't understand, but it sounded accepting.

He didn't fight when Levi and Emily hoisted him into the back seat of the Jeep. She buckled him in, arranged his tail the floor and flinched guiltily when he cried out in pain.

"Sorry," she said. "I'm sorry!"

Levi fidgeted, got into the passenger seat and spent the whole twenty-minute ride turned around in his seat, staring back at the creature.

The more he stared, the more the same word repeated over and over in his head, but he wouldn't say it. It was too ridiculous.

Good Jewish boys from Long Island did not move to California to study Art History and find mythical creatures while watching the sunrise with a lesbian.

Emily drove too fast, and he said, "Slow down. If we get pulled over, this is too weird to explain."

She slowed.

Once home, they walked past the house, carrying the creature as quickly as they could down to the small, private beach surrounded by cliffs on one side and trees on the other. As they walked closer to the sea, he looked up at them, seeming relieved.

Emily's parents were loaded, obscenely, and they had allowed her to live for the past several years in their other summer home in southern California while she went to school. It was a tidy two-bedroom, with a nice lawn and a secluded beach. They preferred the Florida timeshare, though, as they liked to get out of the state.

"And there aren't so many Mexicans," one would say.

"No, just Cubans," the other would laugh.

They slid the creature into the water, and he chortled happily, telling them something. Emily grinned, and Levi smiled, too.

The creature lounged in the shallows, washing the crusty blood from his tail, inspecting his wounds.

Emily watched. "Do you think we should bandage them?"

"I don't know, my mom always told me salt water keeps things clean," Levi said.

She nodded. She crouched beside the creature and asked, "Friends?" She smiled.

He smiled back. He said a few syllables, and she tried to imitate the sounds. He made a noise that was unmistakably laughter, bubbling up from his throat.

"I'm gonna crash," Levi said.

"I'll be in."

He nodded. He showered to get the salt and sand off, knew he needed to vacuum but didn't. He pulled on boxers and got into bed, turning on the fan so it blew a cool breeze over him. It whirred rhythmically, and he was asleep in no time.

When Levi woke up the following morning, he heard Emily on Skype with Charlotte, chatting animatedly. Emily adored Charlotte, every moment they had together. Levi found it endearing, the way they smiled at and spoke with each other.

He pulled on a shirt and pajama pants and shuffled to her room, knocking then letting himself in.

She glanced up.

"You tell her yet?" he mouthed.

She shook her head just a little.

"Maybe not?"

She hesitated, and he heard Charlotte say, "What's that face for? Is that Levi? Turn me around to say hi."

Emily turned around her iPad, and Levi waved at the screen. "You look good, getting lots of sun?" he asked.

She flipped him off, grinning.

"Where's all your hair?"

Her hand flew up to touch her head. She'd shaved off all her hair since the last time he'd seen her. "Oh, well, my aunt's got cancer. We all did it."

"Shit, I'm sorry," he said.

"Yeah, well. We all fucking die."

"I've missed you, Charlotte."

"August sixteenth. Em, turn me back around. Bye, Levi!"

"Bye."

He stepped out of the room, shuffled around for a while, ate some cereal, and yearned for bacon but couldn't have it.

Emily was a vegetarian, and while she had imposed no such rules on him or Charlotte, the smell of meat cooking made her sick, though she tried to hide it. He didn't have it in him to make her sick so he could have bacon.

He shouldn't have been eating bacon anyway.

Once he'd eaten, he looked out the window and down to the beach. Worth a look, he decided and walked down.

He did not see the creature, at least not right away. He found him sunning himself on a rock, maybe napping.

Levi wondered what it was that made Emily decide the creature was a male. His face was a little more angular than the average woman's, but that was about it. No bits sticking out to say girl or boy, no dick or tits or hair to give it away.

He walked a little closer, down to the edge of the water. The creature stirred, then sat up and looked around. He waved.

The goddamn thing waved to him, and Levi had no choice but to go over because when things that didn't exist waved to him he had to say hi.

"Hello," Levi said.

He burbled something, clicking.

Levi pointed to his tail, which looked terrible and scabby. "Better?"

He stared, black eyes puzzling out the meaning.

"Um." He sighed. He had never been good at things like this; charades were bad enough with a common language. He sat.

The creature reached over and plucked at his pajama pants. Levi almost swatted his hand away but figured he was only curious. Probably not a lot of reindeer print pants in the ocean.

A stomach gurgled, and Levi knew it hadn't been his. He glanced at the creature, thought for a moment then pointed to where he guessed his stomach would be.

"Food?"

The creature tilted his head.

"Um...Eat?" He pantomimed eating. "Food?" He mimed again.

The creature nodded and pointed to his tail and said something.

"Well, what do you eat?" Levi wondered. "Fish, probably, right?"

The creature stared.

In the shallow layer of sand between them, Levi traced a rudimentary fish with fins and gills and scales. He pointed and asked, "Food?" and pointed to his mouth.

The creature shook his head, wiped away the picture and traced a much less generic type of fish.

"Picky!" Levi said, amused. He traced a crab.

He nodded and added shrimp.

They spent a little time trading pictures, and Levi found out that this thing ate a variety of sea life, as well as seaweed and something Levi guessed to be fruits or vegetables or something that grew in the earth because it didn't look like an animal. He wasn't sure, but coconuts had to float out to sea from time to time.

He stood, went inside, and came back with tuna, the only thing they had. He had dumped it into a bowl and, curious about the plant thing he had drawn, grabbed an apple.

He returned to the rock and handed over the bowl.

The creature regarded the food for a moment, seeming concerned. Levi pantomimed eating, and the thing tasted what he had brought, then ate it, probably too hungry to care.

When he was done, Levi handed over the apple, and the creature sunk his pointy teeth into it, looked surprised for a moment, then gobbled it down. He said something Levi couldn't understand, but he was gesturing to the apple and seemed pleased.

"Good?" Levi asked, giving a thumbs-up.

The creature imitated his gesture.

"I'm glad."

He burbled.

Levi stared for a minute, thinking. A can of tuna and an apple was not a meal, not for him and certainly not for this creature, who was lean and made all of muscle, almost two feet longer than Levi, though the extra length was mostly tail.

He said, "Wait here," then walked off, to the garage, finding a fishing pole. *Teach a man to fish*, he thought, amusing himself.

"Where're you going?" Emily came out the door the same time he left the garage.

"He needs to eat."

"We're not gonna make him fish for it! He's hurt. We'll go buy something."

Levi thought then said, "It will give him something to do, probably. I'd be bored."

She shrugged. "Give it a try, I guess."

She followed him down to the beach.

The creature waved to both of them, smiling.

"He seems so happy, I wouldn't be happy if I was him," Emily said.

Levi sat next to the creature with the fishing pole, showed him how it worked, explaining the whole time, even though his words were useless. The creature watched intently anyway.

When Levi showed him the hook, he frowned.

"What?" Levi asked.

He pointed to the deep punctures in his tail.

"Fishermen must've got him," Emily concluded.

"Big for a fish hook, though," Levi said, "I'd put my money on a gaff for a lot of these."

He traced a gaff in the sand, and the creature nodded. Levi stared at the most severe wound, where the flesh wasn't just punctured but missing or at the very least cleaved.

Levi baited the hook and cast. He waited, pulled in the line when he felt a tug, and found a crab clinging to it.

"You want it?" he offered.

The creature took the crab and crunched into it immediately.

Emily gasped and covered her mouth.

With flecks of crab shell and gooey meat on his face, the creature looked at her, worried. It held out the half-dead thing to her, and she put up a hand in refusal, shaking her head, unable to look at it.

"No, thanks," she whispered.

He frowned.

Levi pointed between the crab and the creature and said, "You eat."

The creature hesitated.

Levi gave him a thumbs-up and elbowed Emily so she echoed the gesture. Finally, the creature gave a thumbs-up too and finished his food, slurping the meat out of the shell and then tossing the remains back into the ocean.

Levi handed over the fishing pole, and the creature cast a few times, struggling to get the hang of it. He managed to get a few bites and learned after a few losses how to jerk the line to hook the fish and reel it in.

He caught a few little fish but put them back; when he finally brought in a sizable catch, he kept it. He chomped into the back of its head, and the fish went still.

Emily looked away then said, "I'll be back in a little bit."

Levi nodded.

The creature watched her go.

"She doesn't eat meat," he said. "Um..." He pointed to the fish and said, "Meat." He pointed to Emily's shrinking form. "No meat."

He chirped something then chowed down on his fish.

Levi watched, fascinated, as he stripped away the flesh with his teeth and some aid from his fingers and left behind most of the guts and the bones and skin. He tossed the remains into the sea and did not cast his line again.

They sat in the sun together for a while, quietly, staring out at the sea. Levi was hot and started to get sweaty. He wanted to go for a swim. The creature seemed to be of the same mind because he gingerly climbed down into the water, his tail poised carefully, and his face twisting up from time to time.

He winced once submerged, letting out a hiss. He lounged in the shallows, the waves lapping over him. He beckoned for Levi to join him.

Levi shook his head.

Emily came back down a few minutes later, and the creature beckoned her into the water. She tugged off her top and her shorts and joined him, tucking her sandy hair up into a bun.

The creature stared at her.

"What?" she asked.

He said something, but his eyes glanced between her face and her breasts. It was a question, and he gestured to his chest, cupping his hands.

"Maybe he wants you to put your tits away," Levi suggested.

She snorted. "Shut up."

The creature asked something again.

"For babies." She made a cradling gesture.

He reached out a hand halfway then stopped and asked something again, his brow knitted.

"Go for it," she said, nodding and gesturing to her chest.

Levi watched from the rock as the creature poked at her breasts in the frank way a child might explore something. He shook his head and said something that sounded like a joke. Levi came down from the rock to the sand and stood behind them, saying, "I think humans are the only ones with boobs like that, he must not get it."

Emily laughed, moved his hands away after a moment and looked at them, looking at the webbing that went part way up his fingers. She ran her fingers along the thin crest that ran from his forehead down the back of his head.

"You should get your suit, Levi, come in," Emily said.

"No, um...I've got some stuff to do in town."

"Bike or car?" she asked.

"Bike. It's not supposed to rain."

"Be safe," she said, which she always did.

While in town, he bought a birthday card for his grandmother and went to the post office, wrote the card and mailed it right then, knowing it would end up crumpled at the bottom of his backpack if he brought it home.

When he returned home, he handed Emily a newspaper he'd gotten in town. He asked, "Where'd our friend go?"

She pointed to where he was floating on his back, his tail drooping.

Levi wondered how much pain their visitor was in; if Levi had been in his place, he would have been begging to go to the hospital. "Do you think he needs medical attention?"

"I don't know. Maybe give it a couple days."

He sat next to her in the water. They were quiet for a few minutes as she read the front-page article about the truck they had found, with only the sound of the water and a few birds. Finally, she said, "Nothing about him in here, just some guy with a lame story about how the truck got there. Forgot to put on the parking break."

He nodded. "Are you ready for Charlotte to come back?"

"Course I am." After a pause, she asked, "Are you?"

"Sort of."

She nodded. "Yeah."

"Gotta get things back together before she gets home," he said.

She nodded again. "We'll do a sweep the week before she gets back. We've been slacking."

Charlotte did not like change; she liked the same things to be in the same spot. She tended to flap her hands, play with her jewelry, or jangle her leg when she sat, she could speak obsessively for a long time—usually about archeology, which was not the worst thing to hear about, and she didn't get sarcasm a lot of the time. She hated fluorescent lights, hated the noises they made.

"Classic autistic," Levi's sister had pronounced softly when she had visited last year. "Doesn't usually happen in girls."

Levi hadn't known what to say; he had just cleared his throat.

Charlotte had heard her, though, and she had said, "Actually, autism is now considered to be prevalent in girls as well as boys but severely under diagnosed because it presents differently, and in our strict patriarchy, we concern ourselves more with how things affect men than they do women. I'm just lucky I presented enough like a man."

"She's got good hearing," Levi had said, not knowing what else to do.

Emily splashed him, and he flinched. "Hey. You're doing that space brain thing."

"Sorry."

"What are we gonna do with this guy?"

"Maybe you can let him play with your boobs some more."

She splashed him again. "Jealous?"

He tried to laugh it off.

"Really?"

He shrugged and then joked, "Hey, you've got 'em out all the time, a guy gets curious."

She laughed. "Hey, if I was both single, and you know, not a lesbian..."

He shook his head. "No. I like being friends with you more than I think I'd like dating you."

"Really?"

"Sure, you make Charlotte watch all those TV shows and eat that terrible stir fry you make. I'd rather die."

She rolled her eyes.

Their friend came up to sit beside them.

"You always look so happy," Emily told him.

He just smiled.

Levi visited the beach at least once a day, just to check in; he liked to go before work so he had a reason to leave, but he didn't have work every day. Sometimes he would bring the creature new things to try. He liked apples, tangerines, chocolate, and oranges, and he did not care for toast or crackers and hated soda and peanut butter.

Emily spent most of her time on the beach with him, having a blast with the creature, the two of them poking and prodding each other, laughing and horsing around.

He came down on the eighth day and found him and Emily sitting together with a picture dictionary.

"Is that a bowl of spaghetti?" she asked as he came to sit next to them.

"Yeah."

"Stop feeding him things!" she said.

"He likes it!" He handed the bowl over to the creature, who took it smiling, giving him a thumbs-up. "See?"

"He's not gonna like it when it makes him sick," she said.

The creature tucked into the spaghetti eagerly.

Levi grinned.

"Oh, hey." Emily gave the creature a tap on his arm. "Go on."

The creature stared, lowering the bowl and fork from his face. He looked hesitant, nervous even.

"Come on!" she said, grinning.

He nodded, setting the bowl down.

She reached out a hand, and they shook. She said, "Hi, I'm Emily."

"Kato," he said, "H-Helloo."

Levi stared. "Did you name him after Green Hornet's butler?"

"No, that's his real name!" she said.

The creature sat a little more upright, looked at Levi and said, "Hhhi, I'mm Kato." He offered his hand.

Levi grinned. "Hi, I'm Levi." He shook his hand.

Kato smiled.

"He tried to teach me to say something, but I couldn't do it." She made a whistly click noise, and Kato laughed. "You're a good whistler, Levi, you should give it a try."

He shrugged. After an uncomfortable, quiet moment, he cleared his throat. "Em...This is...like...this is a lot."

"Yeah, I know," she said.

"Whattt lot?" Kato asked.

"You!" she said, smiling, "You're a lot."

He tilted his head then resumed eating his spaghetti.

"Have you told Charlotte yet?" Levi asked.

"I've drafted like six emails, but then I thought I shouldn't email anything. You know?"

He nodded. It didn't feel right to talk about Kato, and it definitely would have felt wrong to send information about him out into the Internet.

"So, I'm gonna tell her when I get her from the airport."

He nodded.

She picked up her sketchbook from the rock and showed him. "I'm making a picture. So, she can, you know, have an idea, get adjusted."

"That's smart." He looked at the sketch. "It's good."

She rolled her eyes. "You say that about everything I show you."

"Yeah, well, you do good art."

"He's so beautiful." She said fixed her eyes on the creature. "I could look at him forever."

Levi shrugged. He wanted to agree, he did agree, but he didn't want to say it out loud.

Kato put aside the empty bowl and peered over Levi's lap at the sketchbook. He glanced up at Emily.

"Mmmm?" He pointed to himself.

"Yeah, that's you," she said.

He nodded, grinned and gave a thumbs-up.

"Do you think he'd like Jello?" Levi asked.

"You're really going to make him sick."

Levi ignored her and turned his eyes to Kato's tail. The wounds seemed to be healing. The scrapes and cuts from the window were nothing but scabs now. The flesh had knitted mostly back together where it had been cleaved apart, though the deep punctures still worried Levi. They looked better but still not good.

He jumped when the creature put a hand on him, giving him a thumbs-up, saying, "Bettter."

"Can you swim?" Levi asked.

Kato twitched his tail, flexed it, and then said something.

"You'll be okay." Emily gave his arm a pat. "It's only been a little while."

He nodded.

She rubbed his shoulder, giving him a little squeeze.

"He might be better before Charlotte gets home." She sighed, took her sketchbook, handed over the picture dictionary to Levi. "I'm gonna go shower. I gotta do so stuff in town. A couple hours. Haircut, that kind of shit."

He nodded and handed her the empty bowl.

"Are you working today?"

"Nah."

She balanced the bowl on the sketchbook like it was a tray. "Bye, Kato."

"Bbye, Emilyy."

She smiled and took off toward the house.

Kato took the picture dictionary from Levi and flipped through it. He was searching for something, and when he found it, he tapped Levi and pointed. It was a picture of a man and a woman together, a baby between them and a child standing in front.

"That's a family."

"Fammlyyy."

"Fam-i-ly."

"Famm-i-lyy."

"Yeah, family," Levi said.

"Levvi, Emilyy, fammilyy?"

"Are me and Emily a family? No," he said and shook his head. "She has a girlfriend, um..." He pointed to the man and said, "Man."

Kato nodded.

"Woman."

He nodded again.

"Emily is with a woman. Two women." He held up two fingers and pointed to the woman again.

Kato nodded.

Levi wasn't sure he understood but didn't know how else to explain.

Kato twitched his tail, and it flopped into the water. He moved it slowly back and forth, sending ripples out into the sea. He sighed.

Levi glanced over, but Kato shook his head. They sat together for a while. Levi felt a tug on his clothes and looked over to find Kato pulling at his sleeve.

"What?" Levi asked.

He nodded in the direction of the ocean. "Swim?" He pointed up to the sun. "Hhott."

"Oh, uh..."

Kato nodded. "Swim."

He tugged on Levi once more and then lowered himself into the water, floundering somewhat and wincing. It took him a while to get righted once submerged, and once he did, he held himself up with his arms, his tail only moving every now and again. He beckoned to Levi and nearly slipped under the water to do so.

Levi felt terrible watching him and realized Kato had invited him to swim because he needed help. He had watched him and Emily swim together, always close or touching, and realized she had been helping him, not just feeling up her new friend.

He took his phone from his pocket, left it on the dictionary, climbed down the rock and got in.

Once he was in, Kato nodded toward his shirt, frowning and looking perplexed.

"What?" he asked.

"Swim," he said then added something in his own language, gesturing in a way that told Levi he did not approve of shirts while swimming.

Shirts made swimming hard; he was right. It was stupid, he knew that, too; the clinging fabric did nothing to really hide his body and gave him a wicked farmer's tan. He had not always worn a shirt in the water. It had started when he was sixteen, a neighbor's pool party when his brother had pinched his nipple and teased, "You got bigger tits than Ruthie does."

His shirt had not come off at that party or any outing since.

Kato stared at him, waiting and struggling to stay afloat, probably not sure what he was doing standing there fully dressed on a beautiful, hot day in the middle of the summer.

There was no one to see him, no one except the weird creature they had found, who loved to poke at Emily's chest and play with the stretch marks on her thighs.

Levi sighed but didn't pull off his shirt, just waded deeper, to be even with Kato, who shook his head and clucked in a way that reminded Levi of his grandmother when she didn't like something. He lay back and floated on the water, closing his eyes with a look on his face that said *if you want to be stupid I guess I can't stop you.*

He hated that cluck; it was goading and judgmental and irritating. It was a cluck that had made him cut his hair, shave his attempt at a beard, change his pants from jeans to slacks and eat the cabbage part of her stuffed cabbage. He pulled off his shirt and threw it on the rock, where it slapped wetly.

Kato opened one eye, and Levi knew right away he'd been played. Kato had known exactly what to do to provoke the response he'd wanted. Kato grinned at him, and Levi frowned, huffing. The creature grabbed his hand and pulled him over.

He ran his pale gray, speckled fingers over Levi's patch of chest hair. No one had ever done that, ever, not even his ex. He pulled away.

Levi did not like the idea Kato had pulled one over on him; he didn't think he should be smart enough to do such a thing, to be manipulative. Of course, he'd picked up some of a new language in just over a week, so it was apparent Levi had underestimated his intelligence by a long shot.

When Emily came home, she found them back on the rock. She came over and said, "You finally decided to even out your tan, I guess. Ran into Becca. She wants to do lunch, says to bring you."

"When?"

"Next week, like Tuesday or something."

"She'll flake," he said.

"Probably. But if she texts you..."

"I won't get excited." He looked around for his shirt and found it near Kato. He reached for it, and Kato sent it into the sea with a lazy flick of his hand.

Kato made a face that said *oops* but then grinned.
Emily laughed.

Three days later, on Tuesday, after they had cleared their schedules to do lunch with Becca but had gotten a last-minute text asking for a rain check, Emily and Levi found themselves on the beach with Kato.

Kato was eating Jello, three flavors.

Levi had taken off his shirt, and Emily had not said anything. If she had, he would have put it right back on, and he figured she knew. Emily was a good friend, and she'd had her own struggles with her body.

She was a pear, if women were to be classified as fruit, all hips and thighs and ass, but no tits. It made finding clothes hard—Levi knew, he'd been brought on enough shopping trips. She'd frowned at her stretch marks and pinched her jiggly parts; she still did sometimes.

Kato seemed to have no concept of body image, but he was naked all the time. Levi glanced at Kato, who had lain across on Emily's thighs and balanced a bowl of Jello on his chest. Naked but sexless.

Kato fed himself a piece of Jello and with a flick of his tail, sent a tiny splash of water on to Levi's lap. He smiled again then extended a cube of cherry Jello to Levi.

Levi shook his head.

Kato was not fazed; he offered the same piece to Emily, and she slurped it from his fingers without a thought.

Levi thought he saw Kato give him a look before he lay back down but couldn't be sure. He checked his phone and said, "Aw, Em, did you see what your mom tagged you in?"

"No."

He showed her the picture of her and Charlotte from this time last year on a family trip to the Cape. Charlotte had her lips pressed to Emily's cheek, both looking absurdly happy. "Throwback Tuesday."

Emily groaned. "Ugh, she's so *old*."

"See!" Kato insisted.

Levi showed him.

"Emily."

"Oh, he stopped doing the thing with the y."

"We've been working on it," she said.

Kato touched the screen. "Emily family."

"Aw, that's cute," Emily said. "She's my girlfriend."

"Friends?" he asked, "Is family?"

"No, um...girlfriends, like you know." She made a gesture that simulated something sexual with her hands.

"Em!" Levi said.

Kato nodded understandingly then made a well-known gesture involving spread fingers and his tongue.

Emily lost her mind laughing, and Levi felt a mild horror watching the two of them, deep-seated in his East Coast bloodlines. When they had calmed themselves, Kato looked at Levi. "Levi, girl friend?"

"No," he said.

Kato nodded.

"What about you?" Emily asked. "Do you have a girlfriend?"

"I not." He looked like he wanted to express something else but didn't. He laid back and continued with his Jello.

"Bottomless pit," she pronounced.

Kato snaked his tail around Levi's legs, which he did from time to time, though Levi had never seen him do it to Emily.

"I kind of wanted to go out, too," Emily said. "Like, I got excited."

"We can still go."

She shrugged. "I don't know. It's not the same."

"We can order take out."

"Pizza?"

"Ugh, god, no. I'd rather die."

"Oh, I forgot about your precious fucking New York pizza," she said.

"Well, if you'd ever had decent pizza—"

"Shut up, oh my god!" She gave him a push.

"Sushi," he said after a moment.

"Sushi," she agreed.

"Sushi," Kato echoed. "What?"

"You eat it," she said.

He nodded, set aside his now empty plate, and slithered into the water.

Levi stared after. "Do you think maybe Kato's a girl?"

"What?"

"I mean, you just...decided that he's a boy."

"We could ask."

"That feels weird."

"If he was a girl, he'd have boobs or nipples or something."

"I've never seen a dolphin with nipples," Levi said.

She shrugged. "Do you want to call and order, or should I?"

"I can do it," he said. He knew her order by heart, always the same.

An hour later, they'd gone out to pick up the food, and she frowned at the number of bags they were handed. "How much did you fucking order?"

He shrugged.

"Did you order sushi for him?" she asked.

He shrugged.

"Levi!"

"What?"

She shook her head.

"It's *fish*! He can have fish. He eats it all the time."

"You're ridiculous, you know that, right?"

He didn't say much for most of the ride. They ate on the beach and tried to teach Kato how to use chopsticks. He had no patience for them and ate with his hands, devouring a few rolls then proclaiming, "Good eat."

"Food," Emily said, "It's good food."

"Good food."

"You like it?"

He nodded.

"Levi ordered extra for you," she said. "So thoughtful, this one!"

"Shut up."

"Hey, we should have a fire tonight," she said. "You working tomorrow?"

Levi shook his head, and once he had eaten, he began to drag over dry wood and brush.

Kato stared then asked Emily, "What?"

"Fire."

He frowned. "What fire?"

"You'll see."

He wrinkled his nose.

When the sun had started to sink, they dug a pit in the sand and balled up some newspaper, shoving it under twigs and brush. They piled branches on top and lit the paper. Kato watched, asking questions, and growing plainly irritated when he was told to wait and watch, to the point where he huffed and slunk off into the water, ignoring them until the fire blazed starkly, casting orange light over them and the blankets they had brought down to the beach.

He reappeared then, pointing, and asking, "What?"

"Fire," Emily said.

"Why?" he asked.

He was good with question words, seemed to grasp what they meant sooner than other words. When he spoke, he had an odd lilt to his voice: he put too much emphasis on some words, he clicked a little on ts, and whistled on some of the vowels, but he was almost always comprehensible, using gestures when words failed him.

"For fun," she said.

"Hhott," he pronounced after a moment.

"Yeah, for cooking."

"Cookkingg?"

She nodded.

"What?" he asked. "What cookkingg?"

"Nothing, baby, what's cooking with you?" she answered lamely, a goofy smile on her face.

"*What cook?*" he asked again.

"Go get a fish or a crab or something," Levi said.

Kato regarded him cautiously. "For you?"

"Yeah, for me, come on." Levi smiled at the guarded reaction he'd gotten.

Kato nodded, smiling, then zipped off into the water and came back with his hands full of crabs, four of them. He had, since he'd gotten better at swimming, abandoned the fishing pole. He handed them over to Levi, positively radiant.

Levi wasn't sure why he looked so happy because he'd caught crabs before, but he took them and said, "Sorry, Em," then tossed them on the fire.

Kato looked appalled. "What!"

"Cooking," Levi said.

"*Hhott*," he said, frowning.

Levi had baked crabs like this before with friends at home when they had planned a crab boil but forgotten a pot. It worked. He shoveled some sand over them and moved them to the side of the fire.

He set a timer on his phone, and Kato ignored him the whole time. When the timer went off, he took a stick and pulled the crabs out. He waited for them to cool, rinsed them in the sea and handed one to Kato.

"Eat," he said. "It's cooked now."

Kato regarded him warily then cracked it open, looking at the firmed-up meat, frowning at it. "Nott sofff."

"No, it's cooked," Levi said. "Eat. You okay, Em?"

"Yeah." She looked only a little faint.

Kato ate, picking at it with his fingers, then sat up a little straighter. "Like...ttunnaa?"

"Yeah, like tuna," Levi said, "Cooked. You make it hot, and it cooks."

"Why?"

"People usually don't eat stuff unless it's cooked. Meat, fish, we cook it first, or it can make us sick."

"Ssssickk?"

Emily pretended to barf. "You know, sick."

"Like hhurt."

"Yeah, sick is like hurt. Shit, you're smart," she said.

"Do you like it?" Levi pointed to the cooked crab.

He made a clicking noise they knew meant he was searching for the right words. "Not..." He sighed.

"Different?" Levi asked. "It's not the same?"

Emily traced two circles, then two triangles, then a circle and a triangle. "Same. Same. Different. Not the same."

Kato nodded. "Not the ssamme."

"Different is still good," she said.

He stared at the crab in his hands, picked at it, but didn't devour it with his usual gusto. He picked at a second one but seemed off the entire night.

"What's wrong, buddy?" Emily asked around midnight.

"Wrong?"

"Yeah, you look sad. Not happy."

"Oh." He glanced at Levi quickly, and then looked away.

She touched his shoulder. "What? Is it about the crabs?"

He shrugged, and they knew it was about the crabs.

"I'm sorry," Levi said. "Whatever it was, I didn't mean to upset you. You know, make you sad."

Kato shrugged again.

Levi poked him in the belly, not hard, just teasing, the same way he did to Emily when she was being pouty. "Come on, I said sorry."

"What sorry?" he asked coldly.

"Sorry like...I feel bad I did it. I'm sad because you're sad," he said, reaching out to put a hand on Kato's shoulder, giving a little squeeze, still not over the feel of Kato's skin. It was smooth, slippery when wet, but not rubbery like a dolphin's would be and not entirely human, either. So many things about him were almost human.

Kato leaned into his touch a little, almost nuzzling his shoulder against Levi's hand.

"Better?" Levi asked.

"Better," the creature confirmed.

Levi smiled, and Kato smiled back.

Emily poked Levi in the belly, smiling, too.

"Shut up," he told her, not liking the way she smiled.

She raised her hands in a peaceful gesture.

They fell asleep on the beach. Emily woke before Levi did, and she poked him awake, putting a finger to her lips. She had her blanket wrapped around her shoulders and sand all over her. He felt smothered, and it took him a few groggy moments to realize Kato had wrapped his tail around his legs and was nestled close to him, his face pushed up against his side. Elbows and shoulders pushed into his ribs and something was squeezed tight against his leg.

"You know how you wanted to know if Kato's a boy or a girl?" she asked softly.

"What, yeah, I guess." Levi wanted to rub his eyes but was worried he'd grind sand into them.

She pointed with her eyes.

Levi had to sit up a little to follow her gaze, and when he did, he wished he had stayed asleep or that he would die immediately. Jabbing into Levi's leg and poking out from Kato's upper tail, maybe six or so inches below his belly button, was what was unmistakably a dick, hard and pink.

Kato looked utterly peaceful, still asleep.

Levi started to panic, his heart hammering fast. He was wrapped up; it would be impossible to escape without waking Kato, who would probably think nothing more of this than he did of fondling Emily's breasts and thighs.

"So I guess he's a boy," she said, grinning and biting her lip to keep from laughing, but a choked giggle came out anyways.

Kato stirred.

"I guess he likes you. He's never done that to me."

"It's not funny," Levi hissed.

"Come on, it happens," she said. "Calm down. It's probably just morning wood. Happens to you!" she reminded, crossing her arms.

Kato opened his eyes, blinking, stretching and tightening his tail around Levi's legs, a gentle squeeze, affectionate. He smiled at Levi, nestling closer to him, his head on his chest, his fingers softly playing with his chest hair.

Maybe Emily was right, maybe it had been just a normal morning hard-on, but Kato seemed to have intentions for it, no matter that Emily was watching, or that he was not human and Levi was.

"I need to get up," Levi said.

Kato titled his head.

"Now. I need to get up *now*." He started to sit up.

Kato unwound from around him but not without allowing his hand to linger on Levi's leg.

Levi hurried off. He went directly to the shower, sitting on the floor. Nice boys did not spoon with sea monsters, did not get excited by it; it was simply out of the question.

Nice boys also didn't get sloppy blowjobs from drunk frat boys in the stall of a dorm bathroom.

Levi could only conclude he was not a nice boy and his grandmother would call any moment to disown him, somehow knowing what he had done.

Except, he told himself, he had not done anything. He'd gotten poked and prodded, gotten a little excited, but he had left.

The bathroom door opened.

"Hey," Emily said, laughter still in her voice but subdued by sheer will.

"I'm showering."

"Bullshit," she declared. "Come on, I can feel that Puritanical, East Coast repression from here. Is this gonna be a Jeff thing all over again?"

"Jeff was human!" Levi protested, pulling his knees close to his chest, pressing his forehead against his knees.

"So, I like Kato better, and I mean, I'm not a schlong expert, but it looked pretty close to me."

"Please stop."

"What's a little mermaid dick between friends?"

"If he was a mermaid, he wouldn't have a dick."

"That's not very trans-inclusive of you."

He sighed and sent out a silent apology to all women with penises, the way he had sent out prayers for things he wanted in shop windows.

"Well, what if he was a she, what if there wasn't a cock involved?" she asked.

"What if?"

"Well, would you fuck him if he was a mermaid?"

"What are you fucking on about, Em?"

"I'm just saying, think about if this is really about that fact he's a nonexistent sea beast or because you're still not down with who you want to get down with."

"Em, please."

"I'm just saying, I'd fuck a mermaid," she mused. "If I was single. You know, I also don't even think Charlotte would be mad if I fucked a mermaid right now. How many chances do you get to do that? We could do a threesome..."

"You'll fuck anything."

"Slut shaming *and* transphobia in five minutes? Geez, Levi. Enjoy your shower, I guess, make sure you come down to talk to him about this later, 'cause he's confused."

"He's your pet, you explain it," he snapped.

"Now you're just being nasty." She left without another word.

She was right, but he still felt sick.

Eventually, he washed and made himself shave. He did not go back down to the beach and couldn't find Emily anywhere either.

Pablo, the guy who did the lawn, was outside when Levi peeked his head out the door. He called over, "Hey, Levi. How you doing?"

"Pretty good. Nice day."

"Real nice, but uh...I told Emily, maybe you don't go swimming in that beach today?"

"Why?"

"There's something big swimming around down there. Maybe, like, a shark or something. Under the water."

"I'm not in the mood to swim anyway."

"Yeah, well, you be careful."

"Thanks," Levi said and went back inside.

He lay on his bed, staring up at the ceiling for a while, listening to the lawn mower rev and the fan click and whir for a long time. When that got boring, he ate a bowl of cereal, almost poured two bowls, but took just one bowl to the couch.

He was still on the couch when Emily came home. She waved, and he waved, but they didn't speak until dinner time.

"I'm gonna go eat on the beach." She held a massive salad loaded with cheese, nuts, and veggies.

"Kay."

"What do you want me to tell him when he asks?"

He shrugged. "I don't know."

She frowned. "Do you want to talk?"

He almost said no, even though it would have been a horrible lie. Levi's family was good at ignoring; well, not just his family, his whole town was good at pretending they didn't see things that made them uncomfortable.

"Please."

She came to sit beside him. She reached out to hold his hand, which she did whenever someone was upset.

He sighed.

She asked, "So is it like the Jeff thing?"

"Well, I'm not hung over..." he joked, but it was a shit attempt.

"I can tell you it's okay as many times as you need me to," she said. "'Cause however you are is fine. It's the way you're supposed to be."

"To fuck boys or mermaids?" He was still trying to joke but nothing felt funny.

Her mouth twitched.

Levi said, "I'm sorry."

"It's not about me."

He leaned his head against her shoulder. "This sucks."

She hugged him. "It's fine to be confused. I mean, we're so inundated with this heteronormative shit that...you think that it's default. I did, and I never even close to liked boys. All the ones I said I had crushes on looked like girls."

He smiled. "It's easy to ignore boys if you fixate on girls. Easier. It's just...I'm not done...um, coming to terms with it. I can't, you know, wrap my head around it."

It. He'd said 'it' when he'd meant 'me'.

She tightened her arms and planted a kiss on his temple. "You'll be okay."

He nodded. "Eat your salad." He nodded to the bowl.

After a moment, she took it back up, jabbed a fork into it, and speared a walnut. She crunched down, chewing thoughtfully.

He stood, and she didn't ask where he was going.

Pablo had gone, and he felt it was safe to go down to the beach. When he arrived, Kato eyed him warily from where he tread water. Levi gestured for him to come over to the beach, and Kato ducked underwater.

Levi saw his pale gray body slide through water, not in his direction, but away, toward deeper water. He stayed there for a while, and Levi sat on the sand and waited. Kato glanced back at him from time to time but did not approach. After nearly an hour, Levi stripped off his shirt and waded into the water, tired of waiting.

He swam over to Kato, who ducked underwater and slithered away.

The next time Kato surfaced, Levi had been treading water for fifteen minutes, and his legs were burning. "Kato!" he called when he saw Kato's head and shoulders.

Kato looked over.

"Come on, please! I want to talk."

He did not swim away this time and stayed still when Levi paddled over. "What?" he asked.

"Can we talk?"

Kato nodded.

"I freaked out...um...I was scared." He waited to see if Kato would ask what that meant, but he didn't. "I don't...you know, I don't normally do, well, anything, with anyone. Especially not other men."

"Not like men?" Kato sounded kind of hopeful; it was easy to handle rejection if someone just wasn't into guys. Levi knew the feeling well enough.

"Um." He sighed, wishing he was doing this anywhere but ten feet deep in the ocean. "Yes. I do. I like men. And women. And it's...new, for me. Being with men. And I'm not so great with women either. Urk." He spit out a mouthful of water that a small wave had left in his mouth.

Kato's tail swished rhythmically beneath them, Levi could feel it stirring the water. Kato swam away, but this time to the rock where he liked to lie in the sun. Levi followed, and Kato offered a hand to pull him up when he struggled to scale the slippery surface.

Neither of them spoke, and Kato regarded him seriously for a while.

"Scared," Kato said after a moment. "Of...me?"

"No, not of you."

"Of sex?" he asked, and his tone made it sound like it was preposterous, like being afraid of guppies.

Levi sighed. Of course, Emily had taught him the word for sex; she had probably given him every name, vulgar and clinical, for every body part that could be involved in the process. "No, not...not really."

Kato shook his head. "I...not understand. What scared of?"

Levi's eyes were drawn to what would have been Kato's hips if he'd been human, where there was a slit in his tail, and he pulled his eyes back up. "I've just haven't done much, especially not with another guy." Under his breath, he added, "Or a sea monster."

He could not stop thinking he'd seen a set-up like Kato's on the tails of dolphins, in documentaries about the majesty of the sea. He tried not to compare Kato to a dolphin; he clearly was a man, a person, in a way that dolphins were not.

Kato touched his hand.

Levi ran his other hand through his hair. He looked down at himself. "God, I'm fat," he breathed, staring at his pudgy belly and wide thighs.

"Fatt?"

"Yeah, fat." He pinched at his gut. "Fat."

Kato nodded approvingly. "Fat good."

Levi laughed, startled by the proclamation.

"Soff." He patted Levi's belly fondly then let his hand rest on his thigh. "I teach?" He gave a little tug at Levi's swim trunks.

Levi shook his head, a thrill of excitement and then panic running through him.

Kato nodded, took his hand back, and put it on his shoulder, giving a reassuring rub. "Friends. Levi, Kato, friends."

He smiled. "Yeah."

"Friends good."

"Yeah, friends is good."

They sat together for a while until Levi asked, "How's the tail?"

"Almost better all the way," he said, his tone rehearsed, imitating Emily's cadence. "Home soon."

"Home?"

He nodded. "You and Emily come?"

"Is it far?"

"Emily have boat," he said confidently.

"Oh, making plans without me," he said. "I guess we'll come."

Two days later, after he came home from work, Levi saw Emily dragging a rowboat down the beach to the ocean and then hopping in once it was in the water.

"Come on, he's gonna go home," she said.

"Can I pee first?" he asked.

She rolled her eyes. "Guesso. Pee fast."

He didn't rush, and she had her arms folded by the time he got back. He climbed into the boat, and Kato gibbered happily pulling it further into the water. He kept a hold of the rope, looped it loosely around his waist, and Emily made him undo it and tied it in a slip knot.

He swam a few feet below the surface, a yard or so in front of them, and they paddled after him.

"So," Levi said.

"So," Emily returned, her tone mild.

"We're going to see the rest of them?"

"I can't let him go on his own. He's still not totally healed, not even scabbed over all the way. What if something happened!" she cried.

"And it had nothing to do with your personal curiosity."

"Of course, it does, but I really like him. I want to know he's home safe. We might never see him again."

"Mm."

They paddled for nearly forty-five minutes, following the coast south. Kato popped up to breathe and check on them every so often. His English failed him, and he didn't seem to care, chatting happily with them, unable to contain himself.

He brought them to a large beach that was blocked in by rocky, jagged sandbars and lined with cliffs. Secluded, hard for boats to get to, a perfect hiding space.

Emily elbowed Levi and pointed to a handful of creatures who were adding rocks and dirt to the sandbars.

"They made it," she said.

Levi counted nearly four dozen creatures in different colors and sizes, scattered on the beach and in the water, some of them with long winding tails like Kato's and others with two tails, split like legs would be. He saw several two-tailed creatures with infants cradled to their chests, feeding them, and realized those must be the women. The ones with infants had chests that were slightly swollen in a way not seen on the others.

Emily tapped his arm and pointed. "Levi, *look.*"

"I am looking, Em. I have eyes, too." He was unable to stop looking at the large group before them.

A decent amount of the creatures were paired off or in small groups, some same sex, some not, floating together on the water or nestled on a rock, with their tails twined together. Levi looked away when he realized one couple was doing more than cuddling.

He spied what had to be a family, one long-tailed creature holding a baby, lying in the shallows with a two-tailed one. He smiled, watching the little baby pat its father on his face. He couldn't hear them from so far away, but he wondered if it would sound like a human baby.

Kato pulled their boat up onto the sandbar, where the water was only inches deep, slipped over it into the beach and gestured for them to get out.

Levi kicked off his shoes and followed Emily as they clambered out.

Some of the creatures started to notice them, and they stopped and stared. Kato called something in his language to one of them and a little bit of a ruckus started.

Another male, this one bluish and flanked by a dozen tiny creatures, came up to Kato, putting his hands on his face, staring like he'd seen the dead.

Kato embraced him immediately, grinning, then scooped up several of the children, nuzzling them.

The little ones circled around him, clamoring to be picked up, all smiling.

"Kato, are you a dad?" Emily cried, delighted with the idea.

He shook his head.

The other male regarded her warily.

"Friend," Kato said to Emily. "Danei my friend." He explained this to the blue male, who didn't look convinced.

Kato picked up one of the children. "I watch babies." He introduced the child, saying "This Tl'ald. This Mitz. Prad and..."

He glanced around, looking at all the children. He counted them twice, his lips moving, his eyes darting around.

"Eri?" Kato looked at the other male, eyes widening.

The blue male, Danei, gave a grave-sounding answer, and Kato looked instantly crushed. He let the two children he held slip from his arms back into the water. The children went quiet as the two adults spoke in hushed, hurried voices.

Levi and Emily stared, feeling like awkward interlopers.

A few other adults came toward them, including a female who seemed larger than all the others, longer and broader. The children scattered behind their nannies at the sight of her, cowering.

Danei pulled all the little ones close to him, hissing at them and pushing them in the direction of shore, seeming aware of the imminent violence. The large female lashed out at Kato, beating him relentlessly.

"Hey!" Emily cried out, and the female bared her teeth at her, snarling and shouting at her, holding Kato by the back of the neck.

"Kato!" Emily said, not scared by the posturing of an alpha. She'd grown up with a starlet for a sister, a Hollywood sweetheart for a mother and a soap star for a father; she was not frightened by big personalities.

The female sank her teeth into Kato's shoulder, taking a chunk of flesh with her when she pulled back.

Not knowing what to do, not sure if he should interfere, Levi acted anyway, wrapping his arms around Kato and pulling him onto the sandbar.

The large one spat the chunk into her hand and threw it into the sea beyond the sand bar. She pushed their boat off the sandbar and gave a clear warning, gesturing and baring her teeth at them.

The blue male said something, and she shouted at him, too. He cowered, and she swam away.

Kato touched the gout of blood that poured from his shoulder. "In boat," he said to them urgently, his eyes fixed on the pink tinge spreading through the water. "Get in now."

"Kato, what happened?" Emily asked, still standing.

"Eri...eat. Something eat her. I watch, but..."

"You were hurt, though! Doesn't she know you were hurt?"

He shook his head. "I watch, not in ocean. Watch here." He pointed to the beach. "Wrong place. Dangerous. Get in boat. Now. Please."

They got in the boat. Kato handed over the rope he had held, sliding down off the sand bar into the open sea.

Danei seemed distressed by this, called after his friend, and started to go to him, but another adult, this one green, put a hand on him, shaking his head.

Levi stared at the blood, and Emily stared, too, until she said, "Oh fuck sharks! Fuck, Levi, grab him!"

They clambered out of the boat, grabbing at their friend's arms, dragging him back onto the sandbar. The others watched, and Kato thrashed out of their grip.

"*Boat*," he insisted, just his head above the water.

"You, too," Emily said.

He shook his head. "Eri gone. I go, too."

She jumped into the water.

"Boat!" Kato gave her a push toward the sand bar. "Levi, get her in boat."

"You too," Levi said.

He shook his head. "I go, too."

He wrapped a hand around Emily's arm, but she wrapped her arms around his body, not letting go. Levi hesitated. He didn't want to die, he definitely didn't want to get eaten by a shark, but he wanted even less to watch his friends get eaten by a shark.

He dragged the boat back to the sandbar and pleaded, "Kato, get in the boat. Please, before something bad happens."

He felt like he was going to cry. Kato stared at him, looked at Emily, and the slick of blood tinting the water. He sighed, crawled back onto the sandbar and into the boat.

Danei looked a little more pleased with this turn of events.

Kato sat in the boat, curling his tail around himself, not looking at either of them. Emily climbed in after. "If you get out, I'm getting out, too."

He only glanced her way.

She sat right next to him. Levi got into the boat, giving it a push off the sandbar.

"Well, this fucking sucks." He picked up a paddle, hoping they would get home before anything got any worse.

After ten minutes, he asked, "Are we gonna have to put him on suicide watch or something?"

"I don't know," she said.

She tried to look at the bite on his shoulder, and he slapped her hand away then pushed her hard backward so she fell from her seat.

"Hey!" Levi barked, dropping the paddle into the boat. "Don't fucking put your hands on her just because you fucked up!" He helped Emily right herself. "Are you all right, Em?"

She nodded, but a moment later, her face crumbled, and she cried, hiding her face in her hands and doubling over. Not long after, a strange sound reached Levi's ears, a keening wail that sounded sort of like an injured or distressed dog. He looked up to see Kato crying.

In the middle of the ocean, in a rowboat, with two sobbing friends, Levi considered jumping overboard, just for a moment, because it would be so much easier than dealing with them. It was not a problem he could ignore, though he tried to for a moment, to block out the sound so he could think.

"Em..." was all he could think to say.

Kato moved closer to her, reaching out a hand.

"Hey," Levi warned.

Kato put his hand on her knee, slithering himself closer, then touched her back, saying, "Emily, please, sorry."

She nodded, and he wrapped his arms around her, pulling her close.

"Mad?" he asked.

"No." She wiped her eyes.

Kato cradled her to his chest, coiled his tail around her and murmured, "Wrong thing to do."

She didn't tell him it was okay, but she stayed in his arms and said, "I'm not mad at you."

Levi watched, sort of annoyed they were having a tender moment while he had to paddle all the way back. It took more than an hour, and he suspected they were both asleep after just five or six minutes.

Once home, he sloshed out of the boat and waded to shore as soon as he knew the water would not be too deep. He dragged the boat onto the sand and then trudged inside; it was almost dark and he was tired.

He stripped and curled into bed, not caring about anything but himself for a moment, feeling that after an hour-long solo effort to get them home he was allowed to blow the other two off.

Levi stayed away from the beach for a day; he worked and spent time in town, blowing half his paycheck in the grocery store. He made it all the way to the checkout counter before he saw something that made him wonder if Kato would like it.

Bubblegum.

He purchased it without thinking but forgot about it when he got home and found a car parked in the driveway, one he had never seen before: a deep red-purple sedan.

A man Levi didn't know looked over when he biked down the drive and took a step back from Emily, who he had been crowding as she stood at the front door.

"Em?" he asked.

The man answered, "Hey, I heard you guys have some kind of big shark or dolphin around here, I was just asking her—"

"Yeah, and I told you to get out or I'm calling the cops," Emily said, her voice high and thin.

Levi noticed she didn't have her phone on her, just her sketch pad held tight to her chest, and he knew she would have had to turn away from this intruder to get access to make a call.

"This is a private home, if she asked you to leave then you need to go." Levi leanded his bike against the house, taking his phone from his backpack. "Or I'll call right now."

"All right, listen, sorry. I'm just...you know, trying to get some pictures," he said.

"Yeah, and you're harassing a girl while she's asking you to leave," Levi said.

The man swore to himself and headed back to his car, backing up the drive too quickly.

"You okay?" Levi came over to the door.

"Yeah."

"And about last night?"

She shrugged. "Yeah, it's just...you know."

He did know. She'd had a girlfriend once who had pushed her around, in high school, before she was out. She didn't talk about that girlfriend often and never in much detail, but it had obviously left some kind of impression.

"Yeah." He reached into his grocery bag and handed her a stack of magazines. "All your favorite rags, I thought you'd want to unwind."

She hugged him. "You're the best, you know?"

"Sure, my grandmother tells me what a nice boy I am all the time," Levi joked.

She laughed, tightened her hug. "I've been trying to keep an eye on him, but um..."

"I'll go," he offered.

"Thanks." She took his grocery bags for him, as well as his backpack, brought them inside as he kicked off his shoes and socks and then headed to the beach.

Kato was lying on his usual rock, but on his side, his tail curled close to himself, not dangling in the water. Levi sat beside him and didn't say anything. Kato noticed him after a few minutes and rolled over but didn't sit up. His face on the ground, he looked up at Levi.

"How are you?" Levi asked.

"Not good."

"Figured," he said.

"Dead," he said. "New word. *Dead*. My fault."

"But you're not," Levi said.

"Should be."

"No. We all fuck up. Make mistakes. Do the wrong thing."

"You?" Kato asked, and it almost seemed like a challenge.

"Sure."

"What?"

"Drunk driving," he said. "Totaled my dad's car and broke my girlfriend's arm."

Kato's mouth twitched. He probably didn't understand half of what Levi had said but seemed to understand it as a confession.

"Can I look at your shoulder?" Levi asked, pointing.

Kato touched it, shrugged, and then winced. "Will be better."

"Okay."

Kato scooted closer, rested his head on Levi's leg. "I want go home."

"I know, buddy," he said. "But life sucks."

"Sucks."

"You know, it blows, it's shitty. Things don't work out how they should."

Kato sighed, and Levi rubbed his back. Kato wrapped himself around Levi, arms around his neck and tail about his legs. He didn't cry but sad whimpers slipped out from his mouth from time to time.

They passed several melancholy days like this, until one afternoon, after Levi had come home from work, he'd gotten Kato into the water, and while they lounged in the shallows, a slick, dark shape wormed its way through the water toward them.

Levi grabbed Kato's arm, frightened, but Kato patted his hand reassuringly and said, "Friend."

Another creature, green with dark stripes and male, surfaced.

"Lor," Kato said.

"What?"

"He is Lor. Is friend."

"Oh, all right, I thought...um, I thought they sent you away," he said.

Kato nodded.

He and Lor spoke for several moments; Lor presented Kato with a handful of muscles, smiling. Kato regarded them for a moment, looking like he wasn't sure if he wanted them.

Levi tapped Kato on the arm with the back of his hand. "He brought you a present, that's nice. He must have been worried about you." To Levi, it seemed natural to bring food to a mourner. His grandmother had been inundated with such gifts when his grandfather had passed away.

"He has family," Kato said.

Levi wasn't sure what he meant and didn't have anything to add.

Lor offered the muscles again, but his eyes slid to Levi, uncertain and uncomfortable.

"I'll let you two catch up." Levi gave Kato's shoulder a pat and stood. He went inside but watched from the house with Emily, both of them leaning over the back of the couch and staring out the bay window.

"Hey, um...you know how there're those penguins that make pebble nests to attract mates?" She had her eyes fixed on the pair on the beach, her eyebrows pulled together as they always were when she was thinking.

"Do you mean have I seen *The Pebble and the Penguin?*" he asked. "Yes."

"I think food might be their pebbles."

"What?"

"I think they use food to proposition people, 'cause Kato took those clams—"

"Muscles."

"And right after, they started spooning."

"Okay, I guess that's an interesting theory," he said.

"Well, um, Levi, you've been doing nothing but bringing him food and spooning with him."

"Shit." He sat back on the couch. "Shit." He breathed again. "Fuck, I *led him on. I led on a goddamn mermaid.*"

"Yeah, you did," Emily said, smiling goofily.

He put his face in his hands. He had flirted and then backed out, something universally scorned. He was a tease, the only thing worse than a slut. He told himself he was being unfair, that Charlotte would have reamed him for if he'd shared those thoughts.

"It's not like you knew," Emily said.

He groaned.

"Hey, tomorrow you have to help me start cleaning."

"Ugh."

"Yeah, ugh, but you have to help me."

"'Kay."

"You're the best. Let's watch something. We'll let Kato get his groove on."

Emily and Levi spent the week cleaning, reorganizing the house back to the way it was supposed to be so Charlotte could come home to where she lived instead of a mess. They continued to visit Kato, though they often found him with his friend.

Two days before Emily was supposed to go pick up Charlotte, they went down to the beach. Lor had taken off a while ago, and Kato was sitting on his rock, looking moody.

Emily plunked down beside him. "What's wrong?"

He shrugged.

"You gonna introduce us to your boyfriend?" she asked.

He glanced sharply at her. "*Not* boyfriend."

"You two aren't doing the dirty?" Her eyebrows went up.

"No."

"Oh. Figured 'cause you two were all cuddly," she said with some surprise in her tone.

Levi wished he'd stayed inside.

He shook his head. "No. Lor is friend."

"Hey, can I ask you something?"

"Yes."

"Why did he bring you food?"

"To ask."

"Ask what?"

"Is...um..." He paused to search for his words. "How to get things."

"Like sex?" she asked.

He nodded then added, "Or other things. Get help or to watch babies or friends."

"What does he want?" she asked.

"Sex."

She snorted. Levi cleared his throat. They both glanced at him.

He hadn't been sure he wanted to say anything, but it felt wrong to leave the issue unaddressed. Levi stammered, "Kato, I, uh...I didn't know. About the food, that it was—"

"I know," Kato interrupted. "After crabs."

He felt himself blushing. "Oh."

"Is okay. Not mad."

"Good."

"Um, so, anyway, um...I'm going to bring my girlfriend home soon," Emily said.

"Charlotte," Kato recalled.

She nodded. "Anyway, if you don't want to meet her cause you're...hiding out or whatever, I don't know. Anyway...she's a little different. You can't touch her like you touch us. She doesn't like it."

"No touch?"

"Not strangers."

"Strangers."

"It's when you're not friends yet. She'll really like you, but...she's just different. So don't touch her, okay? And the things she's says might sound kind of weird."

"Everything sound weird," Kato said.

Emily snorted.

"I not touch," he promised.

"Thanks."

Levi sat down, realizing how awkward it was to loom while the other two sat together. "So you said Lor has a family?"

"Yes."

"But he's here trying to get with you," he said. "Is that okay? To be with more than one person?"

"Um...can be. Family has to...uh. Talk."

"Got it," she said. "Do you like him?"

He shrugged. "Tala not okay."

"What?"

"Tala and Lor...together. Tala only want them together."

"Ohhhh," Emily said, understanding what he meant. "All right."

Levi was surprised by the idea that even mythical sea creatures could be cheating scumbags. It seemed as though it should be reserved for the human race, but maybe that was only because Kato, as far as Levi could tell, was a generally decent person.

Kato leaned against her but let his tail rest against Levi's leg.

"Hey," Emily said.

"What?" Levi asked.

"Did I tell you we're—"

"Getting a hotel room 'cause her flight is in at three a.m.? Yes. Have fun."

She grinned, and he had to smile back.

When she left to get Charlotte, she was full of bouncy, anxious energy.

As she left, he could only say, "Drive safe."

She nodded.

The house felt hollow without her, so he went down to the beach. Kato was not alone, and Levi turned to leave, but he recalled how Kato had said Lor was not his boyfriend, so he stayed at the beach.

Kato waved. Lor seemed indifferent and had his tail wrapped around Kato's. Levi was glad he'd brought a book.

He listened to them talk with each other and realized he had picked up the meaning of a few words. Lor seemed to be cajoling, and Kato's answers grew shorter as the conversation went on.

Their voices escalated in volume and became accompanied by splashing; he glanced up, expecting to see them tangled together doing something naughty. He did and immediately glanced back down at his book. He stood, glanced one more time, and noticed they appeared to be grappling more than feeling each other up.

"Hey!" he called. "Kato, are you all right?"

Lor glanced over at him, which gave Kato a moment to slither out of his grasp. Lor pursued, but Kato headed right to the beach, to Levi's feet, grabbing onto his legs. He lashed at Lor with his tail, baring his teeth.

Lor paused when the water got shallow. Levi assumed it was because he knew Levi would have an advantage on land; he assumed this because the green creature had fixed him with a nasty look, treating him like competition.

He hoped he would not have to fight off this creature.

Kato tugged on his shorts, glancing up at him. "Do something," he hissed.

"I...uh." He glanced around, grabbed up a handful of beach rocks and tossed them at Lor. They plunked lamely in the sea, but a large one splashed close to his tail, and he whipped it out of the way. Levi hadn't meant to hit him.

Kato jabbered something at his suitor, lashing his tail again. Lor retreated when Levi picked up another large stone, throwing dirty glances back over his shoulder for a few yards, then zipping off, spitting something nasty-sounding as he went.

"Is he gonna come back?" Levi asked.

"No. You win."

"I, uh, I wasn't—"

"I know," Kato said. "He not."

"Okay. What did he say to you? When he went?"

"I not...uh..." He thought. "Good? I not good enough?"

"Oh."

Kato sighed.

"I'll be right back." Levi hurried up to the house. He came back with Emily's iPad and a couple of blankets and old pillows. He set up the blankets and propped up the iPad on its side; he lay on his stomach and gestured for Kato to join him. Levi rested his arms and chin on the pillow, and Kato imitated him.

"What we doing?" Kato asked.

"Shh." He tapped the play button on the screen.

After just a moment, Kato gave him a weird look. "What?"

"It's a movie."

He sighed.

"Just watch."

"But those...um...look like me, not the same."

"Yeah, it's called *The Little Mermaid*. Shut up and watch it."

"Mermaid."

"You're a mermaid."

"Oh." Kato scooted just a little closer to Levi and settled into the nest they'd created. He fixed his eyes on the screen, stopping every so often to ask a question.

The Little Mermaid was one of Levi's favorites, along with *Aladdin*. He'd watched it endlessly, not just as a child, but through high school.

Kato laughed a lot during the movie. He seemed to find it ridiculous. When Ariel traded her voice for a pair of legs, he snorted. "Tail better."

"How do you know?"

"Crab right, sea better," he pronounced. "I like sea witch. Fat."

Levi smiled.

"Soft," Kato murmured, his eyes fixed on the screen.

He did not like the end of the movie, though, shaking his head and saying firmly, "Not same."

"What?" Levi asked.

"Not same, he at home, she leave family. Not good."

"You're right. It's not fair," Levi agreed. "They live next to the ocean, though. She can visit."

"Legs," he spat.

Levi laughed. "You're a fucking piece of work, you know that?"

"No," he said, smiling.

Levi laughed again. "You want to watch another movie?"

"Mmm. Okay."

"More mermaids?"

"No."

"Oh, wait, wait, I know." He pulled up *The Secret of Roan Inish*, which made Kato cry, not weeping like he had before but sniffling and making small whines from time to time.

He cuddled close to Levi for the film. Afterward, he rolled up onto his back and looked up at the stars. He tugged on Levi's shirt and pointed up at them. "Look. Byouiful."

"Yeah," he agreed. The world felt beautiful just then, for a few moments.

"I like movie," Kato said.

"Me too."

"Good...um...sorty?"

"Story?"

"Mmm. Story."

"Do you have stories? You and the others."

"Yes. Many. Stories...I tell to babies. When I watch them."

"What kind?"

"Story of us. Of long ago, of dead ones and...good ones."

"Kato, you're a teacher," he declared, smiling, tickled by the idea.

"Teacher."

"Yeah?"

"What are you?"

"A student, I guess. A learner. People teach me things."

"Teach what?"

"About art."

"Art?"

Levi rolled over, grabbed the iPad and sat up. He showed Kato paintings and sculptures, cave art, and mosaics, and Kato seemed to understand, listening eagerly as Levi jabbered. After a while, Levi yawned, rubbing his eyes.

"Sleep," Kato advised. "Me too."

"Yeah?"

He nodded.

"I'll see you in the morning, then," he said.

He nodded. The creature hesitated for a moment then slipped into the water, disappearing into the darkness after just a little while. Levi watched for just a moment then went inside.

He woke in the mid-morning and went down to the beach. He had two bowls of cereal and the iPad, fully charged. Kato smiled and waved when he approached. They ate breakfast in a mild, familiar silence.

"I'm working today for a while. Em will be home, though."

"Work."

"Yeah, you know, work. I go all the time."

Kato clicked, his thinking sound.

"Anyway, I figured, you liked movies, right?"

He nodded.

"And, uh, you know, I brought down the iPad," he said. "Don't—"

"Get wet. I know. Like phone."

"Yeah." He handed over the iPad, swiped to open it and pulled up a show. "I watched this all the time when I was a kid, I think it'll help you, like...learn to talk like us better."

"You learn to talk like me," Kato said, slightly accusatory.

Levi whistled two notes, a trilling high-low sound that Kato made sometimes, usually when he was keyed-up about something.

Kato's eyes opened wide, and he laughed.

"What did I say?"

"Is um...bad word. Like...um...Emily says a lot. Fffff....?"

"Fuck?"

He nodded.

Levi grinned, delighted to find Kato swore when he was excited. Kato smiled, too, and whistled another sound, two short highs and then a long low note. Levi imitated it. He'd always had a knack for whistling; he and his mother had whistled duets all the time, irritating the hell out of the rest of his family.

Kato laughed again.

"What did I say?"

"Not what I say."

The creature whistled again, and Levi mimicked again. This time, Kato nodded his approval.

"So what does it mean?"

"Friends." Kato glanced at the iPad in his lap. "What show?"

"*Sesame Street*," he told him. "I got all the old episodes. You'll like it, I think. I have to go."

Kato nodded, looking at him sort of sideways, and for a moment, Levi thought he was going to do something, almost even wanted him to, but Kato turned his eyes back and pressed the play button.

When Levi came home hours later, a red-purple car was parked in the driveway. Emily's jeep wasn't there yet. He took his phone out of his pocket, dialed 911 but didn't press call yet. He went down to the beach, didn't see Kato, but did see the man from last time.

He pressed dial, put the phone to his ear. It was not a real emergency, no fire or injury or armed marauder, at least not one he could explain, but the situation made his heart patter faster, scared the shit out of him, really.

"9-1-1. What's your emergency?"

"Hi, there's a man here, wandering around our house while no one's home. Like, I, uh, I just got home, and he's walking around down on our beach, but he's...he's been here before, while my friend was home alone."

"All right, sir, can you tell me your address and your name?"

"Levi Goldberg, 158 Claremont Drive."

"Okay, and can you describe this man?"

"Uhm, white, light brown hair, forties. He's wearing, like, cargo shorts and a polo."

"All right, and describe his activities?"

"He's on our beach, like...but it's not like he's lost, we have a really long driveway with a big sign saying private property. And this is the second time he's been here."

"Can you tell if he's armed?"

"I don't know."

"Sir, can you get inside your house?"

He glanced at the door. "Yes."

"Go inside your house. I am going to send an officer over."

"Okay, but um...my friends are coming home soon, and one of them has autism, can you make sure you let whoever you're sending know? She gets kind of worked up about stuff, and I don't want anything to happen to her."

"Yes, I will advise the responding officer. Are you inside the house?"

"Not yet," he said. A moment later, he added, "I am now."

"Are your doors locked?"

"Yeah, I just locked it." He went over to the window and watched the man.

"Okay, sir, would you like me to stay on the line with you until the officer arrives?"

"Um..." He did but felt like a pussy admitting it. "Um, no, like...I think I'll be okay, I just...you know, my friend, she's home alone sometimes."

"Are you sure?"

"Someone's on their way?"

"Yes."

"Um."

"I'll stay on the line with you."

He didn't have anything to talk about and felt the need to make small talk. "Um...like, my friend kind of has famous parents, do you think he's like a stalker or something?"

"Well, lots of people in California have famous parents."

"And a lot of them get stalked!" he said, peering out the window, knowing Kato was smart enough to hide from strangers who came poking around. He saw the iPad sitting on the rock, carefully placed in the shade and not in the sand, which sent a rush of affection through him. He was sure his mother would call him 'such a nice boy' and say she was glad he'd made friends with a nice boy.

"Not like that Mike boy you used to hang around with, all those piercings. It's just tasteless," she'd say. He could imagine it perfectly, maybe because she'd said the same thing about Emily.

After about ten minutes, a cop car rolled down the drive. An officer in her thirties got out, and Levi went to the front door.

"You put in the call?" she asked.

"Yeah."

"Have you talked to this guy at all?"

"No, uh, I guess...I don't know. I got kind of spooked," he admitted.

"Your friends still not home?"

"No, not yet."

She nodded. "You stay up here. I'll get him to leave."

"Thanks."

He watched her and something in the water caught his eye. Something was moving deep in the water, in the shadow of the cliffs that surrounded the beach on one side, near where the water of their bay touched the sea.

Kato surfaced, took a breath, and ducked back down; Levi's mouth went dry, and he made himself look back to the officer. She spoke with the man, and he made a lot of deferential gestures. The officer didn't seem satisfied.

He handed over his driver's license, and she copied the information down.

Levi heard her raise her voice at the man, telling him if he didn't move now he'd see jail time. She took the camera from him and bullied him into deleting the pictures he'd taken. Her tone was harsh and Levi normally would have protested her methods, if he hadn't been so freaked out.

The officer followed him. The man sped out of the driveway, and she said to Levi, "If he shows up again, they'll take him in. I hate creeps like him, coming around trying to look at girls and sell pictures."

Levi nodded.

"And I've got his information. If you or your friend want to file a complaint or anything, you can just call down to the station."

"Thanks."

She left after a couple of minutes, and Levi went down to the beach. Kato darted through the water immediately, popping to the surface as soon as Levi's feet touched the water. Kato jabbered excitedly at him and Levi explained, "Well, he's gone now. He shouldn't be back. Did he see you?"

"Don't know."

"Are you okay?"

Kato nodded. "Man is not friend?"

"No." Levi sat down in the water, and Kato came up right beside him.

"You look sad."

"I was scared."

"Scared...of man?"

"Yeah. He...uh, he keeps coming around. I think he knows you're here, and it just..." He felt kind of weepy for a moment but swallowed hard. "I don't want anything to happen to you."

Kato rested his head against Levi's shoulder, wrapped his arms around him and cooed something Levi didn't understand, but it sounded reassuring. It hurt to hear, and it hurt to have Kato wrapped around him. His world had become impossible. He had met a creature that didn't exist, made friends with him, and now he was worried about him, about what would happen and if he would leave or if he would stay.

"Kato?"

"Yes."

"Are you going to stay here?"

"What?"

"With us. Or are you going to find a new home? Are there more of you, like if you went out and found a new family?"

Kato pulled away from him. "Stay?"

"Yeah."

"I...um..." Kato looked out to the sea. "I not know."

"Me neither," Levi said.

The creature fidgeted some more. He clicked and whistled, a trilling high-low. He made the sound a couple times, agitated about something.

Levi asked, "What's wrong?"

"I..." he sighed. "Levi...we are friends?"

"Yes."

"We can be...uh. I know...you said." He swore again. "But..."

"I don't know," Levi interrupted. "Kato, I'm really sorry. I don't know. It's...this isn't, you know...it's not normal! I don't know how this could ever work."

Kato nodded, playing with the webbing between his fingers, swishing his tail idly in the water.

Levi thought about all the ways there could never be anything real between them; they could not live in each other's worlds, they would never share a bed or a home. His parents would never understand, not in a hundred years.

"I know." Kato eyes were still on his hands. "We are not the same."

"I'm sorry," Levi sighed.

Kato shook his head. "Is okay."

Levi reached out and held his hand for a moment. He didn't want to talk about sad, serious, impossible things anymore, so he asked, "Did you like the show?"

"Yes."

"Good."

"Swim?"

"Uh, yeah..." He heard tires crunching down the drive. He turned to see the jeep returning. "Oh, they're home."

Kato looked, too. He chittered something, his black eyes fixed on the girls. His eyes flicked over Emily but stayed on Charlotte.

She was small, short and scrawny, often carded even to see R-rated movies, never able to go to bars. With large eyes and her head shaved, she looked alien, like a fairy-tale creature come to life.

"Remember—"

"Won't touch," Kato vowed. He eyed Charlotte again. "I remember."

Holding hands, the girls made their way to the beach. Charlotte lingered behind, watching, slow and deliberate. She was staring at Kato. Her steps grew slower as she grew closer.

Eventually, she stopped about three feet from the waves.

"It's okay," Emily assured. "Come on."

Charlotte shook her head. Kato waved to her.

"He's really friendly and nice."

Charlotte took one more step then shook her head again and whispered, "I can't. I can't. I can't."

"Hey, it's okay. It's fine."

"It's too much. I can't." She turned and went back up to the house right away.

Emily watched for a second then hurried down to them and knelt in the water. She threw her arms around Kato and explained, "Don't worry, she just needs time. I missed you."

"You too." He hugged her tight.

She stood and headed after Charlotte.

Once the girls were both inside, Kato asked, "We swim now?"

"I don't know. I should go say hi."

Kato shook his head and said, "No. Wait. Um..." He glanced up at the sky and moved his hand across it from east to west.

"She needs time?"

He nodded then took Levi by the wrist and pulled.

"Hey, quit it. Quit pulling on me," he protested, taking his hand back. Kato stopped pulling and pushed himself into the water. "I swim," he said with a flick of his tail. "You stay. I not care." He slipped under the water and disappeared. Levi let out a huff a breath through his nose, not knowing if he should play this game, but from several yards away, Kato's eyes appeared above the water to see if he had followed.

"I'm going to go plug in the iPad and eat," he told the pair of eyes.

Kato splashed him and swam away.

Levi gathered the iPad, didn't disturb Emily and Charlotte, and made himself something to eat. He stayed in for a while, and when Emily reappeared, he told her about the man who had come around again.

Charlotte spent a lot of time watching from a distance. Emily watched with her. Sometimes they went to town, to dinner or the movies. Charlotte loved movies, good or bad. She liked scary movies, with ghosts and aliens and monsters. She called them the remnants of their old religions.

They invited him to go on Friday night.

"Dinner and a movie, our usual," Charlotte offered.

"Uh. I'll stay in. You two catch up."

"You sure?"

"Yeah, I'm not feeling whatever haunted house of the week bullshit you'd be dragging me to."

"See, told you," Emily said, "He doesn't *like* scary movies. Come on." She took Charlotte by the hand. "Besides, I've been stuck with him all year, I want to spend time with you."

Charlotte smiled. "Bye."

"Bye." He waved as they left

Once they'd gone out, he headed down to the beach. The sun had not yet set, but it was thinking about it. He joined Kato on his rock.

"Hi," Kato said.

"Hello."

"Where they go?"

"To see a movie."

He nodded.

Levi held out the iPad. "You want to watch something?"

"No. Um...we wait?"

"Do you want to swim?" he asked, knowing he did.

Kato smiled and nodded. "Yes."

Levi took off his shirt and wrapped the iPad in it, for safe-keeping. He followed Kato when he slid down the rock. The creature took him by the hand and pulled him into deeper water. He always touched when he swam, he did it with Emily too, and Levi wondered if it was how he was used to swimming, if it was normal for him.

He was playful when they swam, too, always circling around and tugging at pieces of clothes, splashing and smiling.

Today he pulled at the leg of Levi's swim trunks from below the surface, pulling him under just a little, enough to get his chin wet and scare him, but nothing more.

"Don't do that," Levi said severely when Kato reappeared. "I told you I don't think it's funny."

"Then take off. Hard to swim with those. Stupid."

"Kato..."

"Not about sex. Just stupid," Kato promised, giving another tug. "Promise. Try it. Please."

He stared at Kato, who did look like he was being honest.

"Come on," he cajoled with the same cadence Emily had when she was cajoling him to do something.

"I don't know how you talk me into stuff like this," he muttered but loosened the string and threw his trunks up on the rock.

"You do because you want to," Kato said. "You like being...um...talk to?"

"Convinced," he said and as soon as the words came out, it felt like a confession, a plea to be convinced to do all the things he wanted to do, but didn't have the guts for.

"Con-vince-d," Kato repeated. He repeated the word to himself several times. "I convince you. You like."

"So?"

Kato shrugged. With a swish of his tail, he glided away. Levi followed after, feeling foolish, but in a good way. It was not too much easier to swim, but he liked the way it felt. It reminded him of being a little kid, of not caring about anything.

The sun set, and the air grew cool on his skin, a little breeze making him shiver. Kato came and wrapped himself around Levi in the water, cradling him.

"Um," Levi said.

"Shh."

"You said—"

"Shh!" Kato insisted, not letting him go.

"You said it wasn't about sex."

"This not sex," he told Levi practically. "I show you sex if you want."

"No!"

"So not worry, huh? Is just...um, touching, it is not matter," Kato explained. "You not touch a lot, you...um, leg things."

"Leg things!" Levi cried.

He nodded.

"Some of us do. I don't. It's not normal where I'm from," he said.

"Normal in sea. Everyone touch. We all touch. Families and friends and more than friends."

"Hmm."

"Emily touch."

"Emily's different," Levi pointed out.

He made a chirp that Levi knew was a sound of agreement. "Levi?"

"What?"

"How much is there beyond the sand? The sea is...big. Very big. The land is big too?"

"The ocean is bigger than the land. And deeper."

"Oh."

"Are there more of you? There's more of us, lots of us. Too many."

"There are more. Lots of families. Um...when it starts to get warm, many families come together. We go um. That way." He pointed south. "Make babies. Well. Not me."

"Yeah?"

"Helps keep...um. Good babies."

"Yeah," Levi said. "Healthier babies."

"Yes."

"You don't like girls? Even a little?"

"No. Tried once," he admitted.

"Oh."

Kato made a sleepy, trilling sound, tightened his tail a little and pulled him closer. Levi realized Kato was keeping him totally afloat. He could have fallen asleep and been perfectly safe. Levi never felt entirely safe in water deeper than he was tall; as soon as his feet couldn't touch the bottom, he began to worry about what lurked in the water around him. In Kato's arms, however, he didn't find himself worrying about such things.

"Do you think...will you go try to live with a different group?" Levi asked after a moment.

Kato didn't seem to like the question because his voice was short when he demanded, "Why?"

"It's just...you're all alone here, aren't you?"

"No, we are friends."

"I mean, there isn't anyone else like you. There's not a life for you here."

Kato uncurled his tail from around him and released him. He didn't do it quickly, so Levi's head didn't slip under, but suddenly Levi felt cold as the water rushed close to his skin and the warmth from Kato's body faded. He had said something wrong.

"What?" Levi asked.

"You want me go."

"What?" he repeated, taken aback by the accusation in his tone.

Kato explained, choosing his words slowly and carefully, "You care we not the same. Emily not care. I not care. *You* care."

"You're right. I do care because this is stupid," he snapped. "There's no way this will ever work. Someone will find you, something bad will happen, and we *aren't* the same. It's not like it's a little different either. You don't even have fucking legs!"

Kato left after that, swimming away faster than Levi had ever seen him move.

Levi tread water for a moment, swam back to shore and yelped when Emily, from the darkness, handed him a towel.

He grabbed it and quickly wrapped it around himself. His hands shook as he did so and his blood burned in his face; he knew he would be flushed pink. He tried to force his thoughts elsewhere, but couldn't.

"That wasn't nice," she admonished.

"What?"

"So what he doesn't have legs. What if he was a human with no legs, would you say shit like that to him?"

"He's *not* a human."

"He's still a person. He has feelings. That's more important than legs. If someone cares about you, that's more important than the labels we put on them."

"So then I'm obligated, just because he likes me?"

"You know that's not what I said."

He shook his head. "You don't get it."

She laughed. "Yeah, you're right, I have no idea what it's like to care about someone who's not exactly like other people."

"Em, don't project—"

"No, fuck you, Levi, you're so caught up with your bullshit about what you should and shouldn't do, you don't realize there's a person who wants to be with you. You've bitched about being single as long as I've known you, never bothered to ask anyone out, and now you've got a real chance at something, and you're worried that, what? You'll have to go to the beach to see him?"

"Em, stop it."

She shook her head. "Fine, I'm done."

She walked away, and he was left standing on the beach like an asshole, mostly naked and slightly sick to his stomach; he gathered up his clothes and the iPad, trudged up to the house and into his room.

Once in bed, he couldn't sleep; he couldn't keep his eyes open, either, but even with the lights off and the fan on, even when he was snuggled into bed in exactly the right way, perfectly comfortable, he couldn't sleep.

In the morning, he was cranky, and he could tell Emily was still pissed at him because she didn't say good morning or tell him to be safe when he went to get his bike to go to work. His coworkers told him off for being grumpy, and when he got home, Emily glanced at him once then turned her eyes back to the salad she was making.

"You look terrible," Charlotte informed him.

He stared at the peanut butter sandwich she had on her plate. He hadn't eaten lunch and breakfast had been a granola bar. She pushed the bread and peanut butter closer to him.

"You need to eat." She handed over the knife and nodded when he glanced at her.

He took it, made himself a sandwich and said nothing.

"What are you fighting about now?" Charlotte asked.

Emily gave her a dirty look, and Levi didn't answer.

"Is it dryer lint again?'

"No," Emily said.

"Emptying the washing machine?"

"No."

"What about—"

"It doesn't matter," Emily snapped.

"It matters what you're fighting about," Charlotte explained. "Or else you wouldn't be fighting."

Emily took her salad and walked away.

Charlotte turned her eyes to him. "So will you tell me?"

He shrugged.

"Levi, come on. This is stupid, whatever it is."

"I just don't want to talk about it, okay?"

She nodded. "Do you want to hear about the Towers of Silence?"

When they'd first met, she wouldn't have bothered to ask, she would have just told him, trapping him in an unending, one-sided conversation. He would still be trapped if he said yes, but at least she had asked consent. "Sure."

She smiled. "Good, 'cause it was amazing. They were used to expose dead bodies to vultures so they could eat them. It's called excarnation, the removal of the flesh and organs of bodies to prepare them for burial."

She paused for just a moment, and he prompted, "Oh, yeah?"

She nodded and waited, tapping her nails.

"Why?"

She grinned and launched into an hour-long lecture on the purposes of different burial rituals in the Ancient Near East, which was, Levi had to admit, interesting and culturally relevant for him.

He wondered which of this information he would remember next time he had to sit shiva, which made him wonder who would die next. It was a bad thought, and he did his best to banish it from his mind.

He ate two sandwiches while he listened and couldn't remember if he'd ever had Kato try peanut butter then told himself he didn't care.

After her lecture was done, Charlotte drank a glass of water then poured herself a soda and one for Levi. She pushed his glass over to him. "So now will you tell me what you're fighting about?"

"She's mad at me."

"I can tell."

"'Cause Kato likes me."

"Is she...jealous?" Her eyes narrowed because the idea was preposterous. He could tell her mind was hard at work; she could dissect ancient cultures with ease, but thrown into a social dynamic that had developed without her, she found herself a little lost.

"No." He didn't elaborate beyond one word, making the choice to let her puzzle it out on her own. He didn't owe her any explanations, he told himself, even though it felt like a dick move.

Charlotte shook her head and fiddled with her necklace, zipping the pendant back and forth on the chain. "I'm going to watch *Ghost Adventures*. You can come."

"No. Thanks."

"You sure? It's not even scary. It's just funny."

"It's not the one with the plumbers?"

She shook her head.

"Okay."

With his soda and a bag of chips, he followed her to the couch. Emily didn't stay for long once he sat down, and he wondered which of them would cave first. Together, he and Charlotte, finished the chips, though he ate most of them, and he felt disgusting for doing so.

He didn't sleep well that night either, but mostly because he woke up in the middle of the night with a cramp in his calf.

His leg still ached two mornings later. Not real pain, just a dull one, enough to remind him he probably needed to drink more water. He lay in bed after he woke up, for a long time, and someone knocked on his door.

He pushed himself up. "What?"

Charlotte opened the door and poked her head in. "I want to meet him."

"Emily can take you."

She shook her head. "I want you to."

He sat up. "Why?"

"Emily...she's too nice. She worries too much about me, and it makes me worry. You don't worry about me."

"Oh, uh...I worry...you know."

She shook her head. "But not like she does. She worries...like, you know, like a mom, not like a friend."

"Oh."

"I know it's because she cares. She does it to everyone."

"Can I shower?"

She nodded and retreated.

When he emerged twenty minutes later, she was standing by the door, and he wondered if she had been there the whole time.

"Where is Emily?"

"Hair appointment."

He nodded.

"She said she wanted to do something different," Charlotte told him as she opened the door.

They both stepped through and headed for the beach. Levi felt sick the whole time, and Charlotte twisted the ring on her right hand, a gift from their second anniversary. At the beach, he scanned the rocks and water for Kato but didn't see him anywhere.

"Do you think he left?" she asked after fifteen minutes.

His throat tightened at the idea, which he felt it shouldn't have until he reminded himself he was allowed to miss a friend, especially one to whom he had been nasty.

"I don't know," he said, trying to fix his face to hide his disappointment, and Charlotte glanced at him.

"Oh."

"Oh what?" He didn't like the way she'd looked at him, like she'd figured something out.

"That's why you're fighting," she told him.

"What?"

"I'm autistic, not stupid. He likes you. Like more than friends."

"Shut up." He hated that his face had revealed so much.

Something beneath the water moved, a dark shadow, long and thin. Charlotte tapped his arm and pointed. He nodded. A pair of black eyes appeared above the surface and looked at him for a little while.

"Come on, get out. She wants to meet you," Levi called.

The eyes disappeared, and he sighed, but a few moments later, Kato came up to the shore and looked up at her.

She was twisting her ring so hard Levi thought she might hurt herself.

"Hi," she said.

"I'm Kato."

"I'm Charlotte."

"Emily's girlfriend."

"Among other things," she muttered to herself.

"Sit," he offered, pointing to the sand next to him.

She sat, cross-legged, pushing her skirt between her legs but leaving a lot of thigh exposed.

Kato stared at the pale golden expanse of thigh, most of which was covered with a tattoo that started at her hip. He reached out, almost touched her then pulled back. "What is?"

She turned so he could see it better, revealing an orange and white koi fish. "It's a koi. My grandfather was a koi breeder in Japan."

"Is fish."

"Yeah, a type people keep as pets."

"Pet."

"An animal that lives with you. It's your friend."

"Oh," he said and nodded.

They looked at each other for a while, until she hesitantly asked, "So...you...they found you in a truck?"

Kato nodded. "They saved me," he explained. "Um...people on..." He thought. "Boat grabbed me."

She nodded. "Sounds terrible."

He shrugged and looked at his tail, which was discolored now in the places where he'd been hurt. "Better now."

"Do you have a family?" Charlotte twisted her ring.

"Not anymore," Kato told her.

She frowned. "What happened?"

"They...um. Told me go. I did something bad."

"Oh."

Levi cleared his throat, and when she looked up at him, he asked, "Uh, so...you're okay?"

"What do you mean?"

"Can I go back inside now?"

"If you want, I guess." Charlotte looked at Kato as though she wanted to confirm the choice with him.

Kato frowned when she looked at him and said to Levi, "I not care, go, you...waste time, anyway. Stupid."

He crossed his arms. Levi wanted to say something mean, but he couldn't think of anything and probably wouldn't have been able to say it without letting out a sob or two. He turned and walked away.

He heard Charlotte say, "Shit, I guess everyone's mad at him. I thought you guys were friends."

Kato answered, "Friends not care about if we not same. Not friends."

That was the last thing Levi listened to; he walked faster toward the house. He slammed the house door behind him, sat down in his room for a minute, but didn't feel any better. He could hear his blood in his ears.

Something needed to happen, and the longer he sat there, the more it needed to happen. The first sob came out more like a cough, forcing its way through his mouth. He tried not to, but cried anyway, curling himself around a pillow and burying his face in it, hoping no one could hear.

He wanted to call his mother, but he couldn't talk to her about this, not about mythical creatures with beautiful faces, ones who liked to hold him close. She would think he'd lost his mind.

Emily let herself in after he'd been quiet for a while.

"Hey," she prompted softly.

He didn't say anything.

"I'm sorry I was mean. I didn't think it would upset you this much. I just thought you needed, you know, tough love or whatever."

He shook his head. "Thasnotit."

"What? I can't...when you talk into the pillow, I can't hear you."

He sniffled and sat up. "That's not it."

"What is then?"

He shook his head. "It's stupid."

"You say to the girl who cried when she turned all her laundry blue." She came over to sit on his bed. "What's wrong? No matter how stupid."

"It's just...he said we weren't friends."

"Oh, Levi," she said, reaching out to rub his back.

"I'm such an asshole."

"Well, you know, you can do the not-asshole thing and apologize," she pointed out. "See, it's what I did when I thought it was my fault you were crying."

"I don't want to."

"Why not?"

"Because I like him. And I shouldn't."

"Doesn't matter," she said. "I promise it doesn't matter. Not even a little."

"I don't know."

"What's the worst thing that can happen?" She leaned her head against his arm. "'Cause either you can make up or you can lose a friend. And so, you know, if you make up, maybe...you know, maybe something will happen. But is that really the worst thing?"

"Yes."

"Why?"

"What would your parents think?"

"They'd think it's hilarious," she said, and he had not wanted that answer.

"Do you want to know what mine would think?"

"It doesn't matter. I don't want to know. And besides, don't make up people's minds for them. I waited a long time to come out 'cause I thought my dad wouldn't be cool with it, 'cause he's...you know, such a good ol' southern boy, but he's been amazing about everything."

Levi nodded.

"So that's what I think, anyway," she told him.

"Thanks. Do you think I could go back to bed and start over?"

"You should try." She squeezed him. "I'm sorry this is all so tough for you."

He nodded. "You changed your hair."

She touched it. "Not really, it's just a little shorter."

"And darker."

"Summer's almost over, time for fall."

"Makes sense."

She patted his arm one more time.

Once she was gone, he lay back down and napped for about an hour. He got up and showered again, brushing his teeth, and putting on new clothes. It almost felt like a new start. He stared at himself in the mirror for a moment, hoping he wouldn't lose his nerve.

He headed to the beach and found Charlotte and Kato still sitting together. As he drew closer, he heard her telling him about all the different types of mermaids that had been represented in ancient cultures. Kato looked a little lost.

Levi stood beside them and cleared his throat again.

Charlotte trailed off and looked up at him. "Hi, what's up?"

"Um, nothing, I just...uh, I wanted to talk."

"To him, not me, I'm guessing," she said.

He tried to smile but didn't think he'd managed to.

"I'll see you later, okay?" she said to Kato.

He nodded but gave Levi a nasty look. As soon as Charlotte was a few yards away, Kato started to slip back into the water.

"Hey, Kato, please," Levi said, "Wait. I want to talk."

He shook his head. "Nothing to say."

"There's a lot to say!" he said. "Please."

Kato hesitated then huffed and scooted back up onto the beach. "What?"

Levi sat, the water soaking into his shorts, then sighed. "I'm sorry I said what I did. About you not having legs."

"Legs are stupid," he said.

Levi waited a moment. "I really am sorry, and I...I know it's not fair to you. But I'm afraid."

Kato frowned. "Of what?"

"That I like you. That this can't work, it's impossible and stupid, but I like it when you touch me, and I want..."

Kato was staring at him.

Levi shook his head. He couldn't say it. "I can't."

Kato grabbed his hand, holding it tight. "No can't. Tell me."

The way Kato gripped his hand made Levi think it was more than just a gesture of comfort or companionship. Kato badly wanted something from him and, from the anxious look on his face, feared losing the chance to have it.

"I don't know." Levi felt weepy again.

Kato touched his face, his fingers wet and slippery, and Levi wrapped his arms around him, pulling him close. His body was so narrow that Levi felt like he could crush him. Kato touched his hair, combing his fingers through it and rested his head on Levi's shoulder.

"Not sad," Kato said, "Is good thing. Happy."

"What if it's not?"

"If not matter. If is not now." Kato pulled back and touched Levi's face again, smiling.

"How come this is so easy for you?"

"Not easy. I have no family. No home. Just this sand and this water. And you. When you are here, I am...not sad. Is better with you."

Levi smiled.

Kato brushed his thumb over Levi's lip and looked at him, unsure, waiting. Levi's tongue slipped out, just for a second; he hadn't meant to, but he tasted the salt Kato had left behind, the tip of his tongue barely touching Kato's finger.

He thought he saw Kato breathe a little faster, shallower. Kato leaned in, and Levi met his lips with too much haste, making it rushed, ugly. Kato tasted like the ocean. They kissed for only briefly before Kato pulled back, touching Levi's face again.

"You are happy?" Kato asked.

Levi nodded.

"Good." Kato kissed him again, this time for a long time. He made a trilling, satisfied coo after a little while and nestled close against Levi. "I am happy, too."

For a moment, nothing felt real, but nothing felt wrong, either; this had to be a dream, something that would bother him for a couple days when he woke up, but just a dream.

There was nothing to say, and Kato seemed content with the silence, but something nagged at Levi, something he couldn't name. School was starting soon. Maybe that was it. It wasn't. There was something else.

"Hey," he said suddenly, and Kato looked up.

"What?"

"I'm supposed to go home. Next month."

Kato looked at him. "This...is this your home?"

"No, um, my real home, where my parents are. It's a holiday. My grandmother will kill me if I don't. I already tried to get out of it 'cause it's after classes start."

Kato frowned. "I not understand."

Levi sighed. "Which part?"

"Where is your home? What is holiday? And classes?"

"I live on the other side of the country."

Kato shook his head, his face scrunching up like he was close to tears.

In the sand, Levi traced an outline of the U.S. and pointed. "This is where we are. This is where I'm from, it's where my family is."

"Far away."

"Yeah."

"You stay there?" The creature looked nervous, almost frightened.

"No, just for a few days."

Kato nodded. "Holiday?"

"When you get together with everyone to celebrate, you know, to have a good time or to remember something important."

"Oh. We have."

"Yeah? Like what?"

"Um...the...uh." He pointed to the sky. "Little...when dark." He sighed, swore and jabbered in frustration for a moment. "Little things up there."

"Stars," Levi said, smiling.

"What?"

"Stars, they're called stars. That's the sky, and the little lights are stars."

Kato wrinkled his nose, which was small, flat and, to Levi, adorable.

"What?"

"Not fair," he said, "I learn everything. You learn nothing."

"I'm sorry, but I think you're smarter than me anyway."

He snorted.

"What?"

"Smart."

"It's when you know a lot, or you're good at figuring things out. It's a good thing."

Kato shrugged.

"And I can't make the noises you make," he said. "When you click? I can't do that."

Kato pressed his lips together for a moment then touched Levi's throat. "From here."

"Yeah, I can't."

Kato's fingers poked into the soft tissue of his throat, looking for something, feeling along the sides. He frowned.

"What?"

He took Levi's hand and placed it on the side of his throat, where he could feel a long, smooth something under the skin. It was not an Adam's apple, that was clearly visible to the left, in the center.

"No, I guess I don't have one," he said.

Kato clicked while Levi's fingers were still touching his throat and whatever it was beneath the skin vibrated. He pulled back, startled, and Kato laughed.

"What else you not have?" he asked.

"Probably lots of things." He picked up Kato's hand and showed him the webbing there. "I don't have that. Haven't got one of these." He touched the ridge on his head. "Or one of those." He pointed to his tail.

"No," he said. "Legs."

"Which are stupid, right?"

Kato nodded, studied him for a while. "Where...um. No." He shook his head.

"What?"

"Not important."

"Okay." He looked down at his legs. "Hey."

"What?"

"How come you have one tail but the girls have two tails?"

"Um...sometimes girls have one tail but...not good for babies. Is..." He made a gesture with his hands that Levi couldn't interpret.

"What? Um, do they get stuck?"

He shook his head and something. "Not make them?"

"Oh, they can't, okay," he said.

Kato nodded. "Can't. Right." He sighed.

"You know, um, you can...you know, if you want, I can try to learn. Maybe I won't be able to say anything, but I'll be able to understand."

He shrugged.

"Okay, well, don't be mad, but I have to go to work later."

"Work," the creature scoffed.

"You say that every time."

"You go do things, make money, but what is money?"

"You buy stuff." He thought for a moment. "Like when people give you food, you get stuff, right?"

He nodded.

"Money's like that, but you can't eat it."

"Oh. What you get with money from work?"

"Food, mostly."

Kato frowned. "Why you not...get food?" He pointed to the ocean.

"It doesn't work like that, we eat a lot of things that don't come from the ocean."

"And you can't take? You have to get with money?"

"Yeah, you have to buy it."

"Why?"

"Because it belongs to someone else. Someone who took the time to make it or catch it. And besides, you can buy other stuff."

"Like what?"

"Like the iPad, that costs money."

"Oh."

"Do you want me to bring it down?"

He nodded.

"Ok."

"Um...we watch before you go?"

He nodded. "Sure."

He had time before work. He got the iPad, and they watched a short documentary about dogs, which Kato really enjoyed, asking a thousand questions about them. Levi showed him how to search for things on Netflix and typed "dog" into the search bar.

"Now all of these should be about dogs," he said.

Kato nodded, flicking through the choices.

"I have to go."

Kato nodded. Levi stood, but Kato grabbed him by the hand and tugged him back down.

"What?"

The creature left a kiss on his mouth. "Now go."

Levi smiled. He went inside to change out of his wet, sandy clothes, and Emily cornered him in his room, halfway dressed.

"I saw that," she said.

"Fuck off," he told her but smiled.

"Good for you."

"I like your hair, did tell you?" He pulled on the last of his clothes. "He has the iPad, but, you know, check on him?"

She nodded.

"And if the guy with the camera comes back—"

"I'm calling the cops, for sure," she said.

He nodded.

"Bike?" she asked.

He nodded again.

"Be safe."

"Thanks."

For the week leading up to the start of the semester, things happened in mostly the same way. If Levi worked, he left Kato with the iPad, sure that Emily or Charlotte would also be down to visit him. If he wasn't working or running errands, he was at the beach. He ate there and brought Kato food, too.

"It's just food. I'm not trying to get anything," he clarified at the end of the week, not sure if Kato's expectations had changed with the situation.

Kato looked up, already halfway through the bowl of pasta. He nodded.

"Shit, he really can eat, can't he?" Charlotte said.

"I think it's probably...like, you know, he has to swim all the time, it's more work." Emily thought for a minute. "Hey, are you going to be all right when it's colder?"

He shrugged then nodded, his mouth full.

"I still don't think you should be feeding him human food," Emily said to Levi.

"If it was going to make him sick, he'd be dead already."

Kato glanced between the two of them. He chewed for a moment more, swallowed, and said, "Don't fight. I don't like it."

"*Sesame Street*'s really paid off," Charlotte said.

"I got him some apps, too, like the ones for kids? Um...the one Jenna loves. *Starfall*," Emily said.

Levi glanced over. "So can you read yet?"

Kato shrugged.

"What's wrong?"

"You go to classes soon?"

"Yeah," he said.

"All day?"

"Not...I mean, for a while, sure."

"And work?"

Levi nodded. "Yeah and work."

Kato sighed.

"Hey, people maintain social lives outside of work and classes," Levi assured.

Kato shook his head. "But I have...nothing all day."

"Oh," Levi said. He hadn't thought of that.

"What did you used to do?" Charlotte asked.

"Watch little ones and teach them."

"Have you tried going back?" Charlotte asked.

Kato shook his head vigorously. "No, Manit already made me go once. I don't know what she do...um...next time."

He touched the mouth-shaped scar on his shoulder.

"Is she like your leader?" Charlotte asked.

He nodded. "Biggest. And strongest. And I let something eat her baby."

"Oh, well, shit." Charlotte twisted her ring. "That sucks."

Kato sighed.

"So wait, what did you teach them?"

"About us," he said.

"Would you tell me?" she asked. "Even just a little? Anything you can. The implications of an oral history from another sentient species are vast. I can't believe I never considered it. Do you have religion?"

"What?" he asked, frowning.

"I think you're going too fast," Emily suggested.

She nodded but didn't seem to really hear. "Religion is a system of beliefs and teachings that are highly valued, considered sacred. Usually, it has social rules, moral codes—"

Kato whistled through his nose, frustrated. "I can't."

"Charlotte, give it a second, okay?" Levi said.

"I just—"

Kato shook his head. "No. I can't. I have the wrong words."

Levi reached out to touch his arm, but Kato pulled away.

"I, uh...I want to swim," he said. "But...to think?"

"Yeah, of course," Levi said.

Charlotte frowned, and Emily fidgeted uncomfortably as Kato slipped into the water and darted away.

"I, uh..." Charlotte stared after him. "I didn't mean to upset him."

"I think he misses home," Levi said. "And, I mean, he can't go back."

She toyed with her necklace. "Should I...you know...?"

"He'll come back," Emily said. "You try again. Slower this time."

Charlotte nodded then sighed.

They finished their lunch, cleaned up, and brought everything inside. Charlotte checked anxiously out the window every five minutes, and when Kato came back a half hour later, she had been standing in front of the window for twenty minutes, bouncing on her toes.

She left as soon as she saw him.

Emily took a step to follow after her, but Levi put a hand on her arm. "She's fine."

Emily sighed. "I just worry."

"I know," he said and then added, "And she knows, too. You know...I get that she's got her differences from most people, but she's not breakable, not over stuff like this."

She shrugged, giving him a look that told him it had been a stupid thing to say. "Doesn't matter, I'm a worrier. I worry. I can't help it. I'd worry if she wasn't on the spectrum."

"They're fine, though, look." He nodded toward the window, where they were both sitting in the sand, talking.

They stayed out there for a while, or at least, she stayed out there. Kato had little choice as to where he could go. Levi and Emily watched them from the window, bitched about classes starting and shared chips and salsa.

"Do you think maybe it's too dangerous for him to go out and be alone?" she asked, "Like that's why he stays here?"

He thought about it for a moment. "Maybe. Whales and stuff usually travel together, right, and seals?"

She nodded. "I think our Tuesday-Thursday classes are at the same time."

"Yeah. Friday classes?" he asked.

"Never!"

"Yeah me neither. What about her?"

"Mostly Monday-Wednesday. One Friday, one of the long ones, at night."

"Ugh."

"Right? You know how Mandy is a bio major, and she has those super long labs? I could never."

"You have long classes, too."

"Yeah, but I *like* doing art stuff."

"So maybe Mandy likes doing biology stuff."

She rolled her eyes. "Shut up."

They watched out the window for a while longer. The conversation between Kato and Charlotte seemed balanced.

"She must be driving him up a wall with the questions," Emily said.

"I don't think he minds. I mean he worked with kids. He must have patience."

"Explains why he put up with your pussyfooting."

He scowled but then ran a hand through his hair.

She reached over and fixed a few dark curls. "You always fuck up your hair. And you need a haircut."

"Ugh, thanks, Bubbe," he said.

"You should get more off the back and sides than the front. I know you always tell them to just take off a few inches, but tell them to make it shorter on the back and sides," she said. "It'll look better."

"Are you saying my hair doesn't look good?" he asked, mock-offended. He was under no illusions what his hair looked like: a mess, much like the rest of him.

"I'll take you tomorrow."

He sighed.

"Shut up," she said, and he knew tomorrow she would be taking him for a haircut, probably to where she got hers done, a place he had walked by and waited outside of but never entered. Maybe she would tell the hairdresser what to do, which would be easier for him.

She dipped a chip into the salsa, taking a large scoop, and crunched thoughtfully for a moment.

"You're not going to make me look stupid, are you?" he asked.

"What? No, I know what I'm doing."

"I just mean...like it won't look like...um, you know, like I'm trying, will it?"

"Trying what?"

"To be cooler than I am. You know, you can't just put a nice hair cut on a schlub and call it a day."

"You're cooler than you think, Levi," she assured, which made him assume he would end up with a haircut that would look good on a skinny or fit guy but mildly ridiculous on him. It would grow out, he assured himself.

"I'm not," he said, and she scoffed.

She ate another chip, and he did, too.

"Are you bored yet?"

"So bored."

"Do you want to see what's on TV?"

"Sure," she said.

They turned to face the TV and spent the rest of the night watching nonsense on the History Channel.

The next morning, she woke him up, hurried him through the shower and drove him into town, parallel parking perfectly in front of her hairdressers.

"Don't I need an appointment or something?" he asked, hesitating before going through the door.

"I already called," she said like he was stupid.

He pressed his lips together and followed her inside, assaulted by the smell of hair and nail products. After a few moments, a woman came over to them, greeted Emily, and surveyed him.

She touched his hair immediately. "God, what great hair. Come on over, what's your name, hon?"

"Levi."

"So what are we doing with you today, Levi?" she asked.

He glanced desperately at Emily, who was right behind them. She and the hairdresser had a ten-minute chat about what to do with him while he stood helplessly.

When they were done, Emily squeezed his arm. "See you in like a little while."

He nodded.

The hairdresser washed his hair, asked him a million questions, took him to a chair and started cutting, all the while asking him things, talking to him like they were old friends. He stammered answers to the questions as best he could and tried to say something like "oh, yeah?" or "I know, right?" to all of her statements.

"So you're not from around here," she said.

"No, uh, Long Island."

"Where about?"

"Merrick." He didn't expect her to know where it was.

"Is that over near Garden City?"

"Uh, yeah, kind of."

"My husband is from Garden City."

"Yeah, really?"

"Sure, he moved out here wanting to be an actor. Well, he's not!" She laughed. "But I think he likes being a plumber more than he ever would have liked acting. I'll tell you something, every time I see an actor, they look miserable."

"Mhmm."

"Okay, close your eyes, hon," she said, and he obeyed.

After what felt like a very long time of cutting and styling, she turned him around and asked him what he thought. He said he liked it, which he would have said regardless of how he felt.

He paid and tipped; Emily was waiting outside for him. She grinned as soon as she saw him. "Levi!"

"What?"

"You look really nice," she said, smiling.

He touched the back of his head, where the hair was cut shorter than it had been since his mother stopped deciding his haircuts for him. "You think?"

"Shut up, yes!" She smacked him the arm. She held out an iced coffee to him. "Try it. It's Oreo flavored."

He tried it. "Oh my God."

"I know, right?" she said. "Anything else you need to do?"

He shook his head, and she brought him home. Once home, he glanced immediately at the beach, and she smiled. "Go ahead, I'm not stopping you."

He blushed.

"I might be down later. I'll make sure I'm really noisy so I don't sneak up on you," she said, grinning.

He kicked off his shoes, peeled off his socks, and went to the water. Kato was there right away.

"Come swim," Kato said.

Levi obliged, tossing aside his shirt, and wading in. He had left his phone with his shirt and had already put on swim trunks in the morning. They had been a staple lately, rotating through the same three pairs and a few pairs of board shorts, the only difference between the trunks and the shorts were the shorts reached a lower past his knees. No jeans or cargo shorts: he'd gotten wet in them once and regretted it for the entire swim.

Kato pulled at the shorts.

"Come on, don't start already. I'm not even in yet."

Kato surveyed him for a moment then said, "Hair is not the same."

"No, I got it cut."

Kato whistled something then took Levi by the hand and pulled him into deeper water.

"I like." Kato ran his hands over the back, touching the curls that remained longer on top. He smelled his hair. "What is smell?"

"Oh, just, like…um, we put stuff in our hair to make it stay the way we want."

Kato shook his head. "Different than before."

"Normally I don't. I probably won't again. The lady did it for me."

"Oh."

"What did you learn today?" he asked.

"Beers…no, um…" He sighed. "Beards? Like dogs."

"Bears?" he asked.

Kato nodded. "Bears," he repeated. "Close eyes and…um…" He touched his nose. "Hold breath."

"Why?"

"Do it."

He closed his eyes and held his breath, and Kato pulled him underwater, running his hand vigorously through Levi's hair for about fifteen seconds. He released him, and Levi popped back up.

"What was that about?"

"Smell was different. It is better now."

Levi smiled. "What if I liked it?"

"You didn't do before, you said won't again," Kato said practically. He circled around Levi for a moment then came closer and pressed his mouth to Levi's, soft and just for a moment. His hands trailed along Levi's arms, and he took his hands, holding them tight. He swam backward a little. "Come."

"Where?"

"Come with me," he said. "I show you something."

"Show me what?"

Kato shook his head. "You can't know yet."

He let go of Levi's hands and swam away, staying close.

Levi followed him but hesitated when they neared the entrance of the cove. "Uh, Kato?"

"What?"

"I don't think I can go out there."

"Not far, I keep...um. Safe. I keep you safe," Kato vowed, taking his hand again and giving a reassuring squeeze.

Levi's gut told him not to go, as did his head and all his other senses. But Kato's hand pulled him forward, and he followed, about ten yards outside of the entrance, then was brought a little while south.

"Come see," Kato said. "Hold breath."

"See what?"

"Underneath."

"Oh."

Kato slipped under, his tail the last to disappear, and Levi followed because he was afraid not to. The water was not very deep, but he could not make it as far as Kato could. After a little while, he tugged on Kato's fin and pointed upward, tapping his chest.

Kato swam right up to him and kissed him, open-mouthed, prying open Levi's lips. Levi seized up, panicking, sure something terrible was going to happen, but Kato only blew a small breath of air into his mouth, resting his hand on his chest. He pulled back, checking Levi's face, giving a questioning thumbs-up.

Levi shook his head, and Kato, holding him close, brought him directly to the surface. Once they had surfaced, Kato touched his face, checking his eyes then putting an ear to his lungs.

"What is wrong?" Kato asked.

"I panicked."

"Why?"

"Because I couldn't breathe!"

Kato pushed the wet curls out of his face. "I give air."

Levi shook his head.

"Why no?"

"Just...I don't. I don't know."

"Scared?" It didn't feel like a jab or a goad.

Levi nodded.

Kato held his face between his hands for a moment, smiling a little bit. Levi almost pulled away, uncomfortable with the tender way Kato looked at him. He shouldn't have been, but no one had ever really looked at him the same way Kato did.

"Try again?" Kato asked, and when he saw that Levi was about to refuse, he addded quickly, "Here, not under."

Levi hesitated. He didn't want to try again, but he also didn't want to be a wet blanket. He wanted to see whatever it was Kato wanted to show him.

"Okay."

Kato pressed his mouth against his again, blowing in air, and this time, Levi had enough presence of mind to breathe in.

"Good?" Kato asked.

Levi nodded.

Kato moved in again, touched his lips to Levi's, but this time, he shared no air, just twined his tail around Levi's legs, pulling him close. Levi's heart quickened, and he felt almost dizzy as he clung to Kato, overwhelmed by the size of the ocean around him, thrilled to have someone pressed close. The creature pulled back after a minute.

"Ready?"

"Okay."

Kato took Levi's hand again and brought him back underwater, holding on to him the whole time. He shared air with Levi three times on the way down and then once more as he showed Levi two huge vertebra, lashed together with thick ropes.

A few bubbles escaped his nose as Levi studied it as best he could, reaching out to feel for what his eyes couldn't make out. The bone had markings carved into it, though he couldn't tell what they meant.

His lungs started to ache and more bubbles slipped out. Kato put a hand on his chest and gave him more air. He looked at the bones a while longer then looked at the surface, feeling a strong need to breathe on his own.

Kato nodded, took his hand, and brought him up. He gasped for air like a fish on land as soon as his head broke the water. Maybe, with a lot of practice, he could learn to do it for longer, but not today.

Once he had caught his breath, he asked, "What are those?"

"Um...from whale? The um..." He touched his own back.

"Back, yeah, I know, but what are they? Where did they come from?"

"Us," Kato said. "We...keep them."

"What are they for?"

He shrugged. "I don't know. No one knows anymore."

"Oh."

"Um...we have sorty–story. We have story that says we were...better, smarter. Long ago. Before..." he trailed off, glanced guiltily at Levi and continued, "Before the boats. There were only some boats before, but now there are lots. More boats, less of us."

Levi stared.

"We are...not as many. There were whole..." He made a shape with his hands, a sort of circle. "Land and water all around."

"Islands."

"Whole islands where we lived. Not now. Now, we...hide. Mostly. And die," he said. "Places that were good now...we die when we go. The water is bad."

"I'm sorry."

Kato frowned. "Why?"

"Because it's our fault. We made it that way. The boats are ours, and we made the water bad and all the garbage that's in here!"

"I know," he said. "But, uh...not because of *you*. Not because of Levi."

Levi sighed. He recycled, he biked when he could, and made sure he turned things off when they weren't in use, but he didn't think Kato understood the impact of the human species on the world. They hadn't just polluted enough to leave behind garbage and poison, they'd polluted enough to change the atmosphere and melt the ice caps.

Kato touched his cheek. "Home?"

He nodded. "Sounds good."

"Sounds good," Kato repeated, then said something to himself in his own language, something mocking.

"Hey," Levi said, "I don't make fun of the way you sound."

"What?" Kato glanced back.

"I heard you. I mean, I didn't get all of it, but it wasn't nice."

Kato stopped and stared for a minute then pecked Levi on the cheek, smiling.

"Home," he said decisively, pulling Levi along the whole time.

When they arrived at the beach, they found Emily and Charlotte frowning at them. Emily with her arms crossed, and Charlotte twisting her ring ferociously.

Emily smacked him as soon as he stood up.

"Where were you!" Emily demanded. "I thought you'd fucking drowned or something."

"Drown." Levi rubbed his arm where she'd hit him.

"Don't hit people," Charlotte said, her voice small.

"I thought I was gonna have to call the cops or something."

"I'm sorry," Levi said.

Kato watched from the sand, his eyes flicking between all of them. He touched Levi's calf and Emily's knee. "I wanted to show something."

She glanced down then knelt. "I'm not mad at you."

"Show him what?" Charlotte asked before anyone could say anything else.

Kato glanced up, straightened himself so he wasn't quite as close to the ground. "Um..."

With his hands, he tried to approximate the shape of what they'd seen.

"It's like a pillar, or...a monument or something," Levi said for him. "Two vertebrae with carvings."

"What!" she said, "You have to show me."

Kato shook his head. "Too deep for you."

She frowned. "Why for me and not for him?"

"I, uh." He touched his mouth. "Shared air with Levi."

She looked at his mouth for a second, put her fingers to her own lips, and then asked, "What if I gave you a camera?"

"Camera?"

"To take pictures with. You know what pictures are."

He nodded.

"If I give you a camera will you take pictures for me?"

"Um, cameras like phone? Can't get wet?"

She shook her head. "I'll find one that can."

He nodded. "I make pictures."

She smiled. "Thanks."

He nodded. "Uh...you wel-come."

"Your."

"Your wel-come," he said.

She nodded.

Emily gave Levi a nasty look. "I'm still mad at you for scaring me," she said but left it at that. "I came down to tell you we're ordering pizza."

Levi made a face.

"Then don't have any!"

"Pizza?" Kato asked.

"It's food," Emily said.

He nodded.

The semester started, and a few days after that, Levi got on a plane for JFK, where his father would be waiting for him, and maybe his brother, too. Kato had given him a very long kiss goodbye, and Emily had driven him to the airport, promising she would let him know how everyone was doing.

On the plane, his long legs touched the back of the seat in front of him, and he found his own seat too narrow to sit comfortably. The food was edible, but not delicious, and the woman sitting next to him smelled a lot like vanilla body spray.

He tried to listen to his iPod, but the ear buds made his ears hurt after a while. When he landed, he was agitated and searched nervously for his father as he wandered through the terminal, herded along with all the other passengers.

"Hey!"

He looked around and saw his father, about fifty pounds lighter than he had been over winter break. He walked over, and his father hugged him.

"Hi, bud. How've you been?"

"Pretty good, Dad. How're you? You look...uh, you know, you look great."

"Thanks, started doing this thing at the gym. Your mother got me into it."

Levi stared, knowing he couldn't have possibly heard right. "What is it?"

"That dance thing."

"Zumba?"

His father nodded.

Levi frowned, trying to imagine having the will or ability to do Zumba, let alone having to do it with a prosthetic leg, as his father did. His plane had left California, but along the way it must have slipped into an alternate time stream.

"Well, I'm glad it's working out."

His father nodded. "Come on, let's get you home. Bubbe's waiting for you."

Levi smiled and took his phone from his pocket, turning it back on. He had a text from Emily and one from Charlotte, both with more emojis than words.

"You kids are addicted to those things," his father said.

"Sorry." Levi put his phone back in his pocket.

The ride from JFK to Merrick was quiet and a little strange. They stopped for bagels, and his father said, "Don't tell your mother. She's got me on a diet."

Levi promised he wouldn't, stuffing his mouth with real food for the first time in months.

He wished somehow the could reconcile life between California and Long Island, feeling deeply content as he devoured an everything bagel with cream cheese and lox.

When he walked inside, his mother and sisters hugged him, his brother nodded at him, and his grandmother kissed his cheeks and held his face between her hands while he hunched over so she could reach him. By the time she released him, he'd been reassured of what a good boy he was and told he'd gotten a very nice haircut.

"I'm sure Emily picked it out for him," his mother said.

He rubbed the back of his neck.

His grandmother nodded and asked, "Are you ever going to let us meet your girlfriend?"

"Bubbe, I told you, she's not my girlfriend. She doesn't even like boys."

His grandmother dismissed his protest with a wave of her hand. He checked his phone when it dinged, and he saw Emily had sent him a series of hearts with a dolphin next to it. He smiled, and his sister Ruth peered at his phone.

"If she's not your girlfriend, why is she texting you hearts?"

"Because she's nice." He put his phone back in his pocket.

"Go get washed up. We're going to eat soon," his mother said.

He nodded and went, leaving his backpack on his bed and looking around his room. It was clean, neat and untouched. He knew they'd been using his closet to store seasonal items, but other than a few extra boxes, things were as they had been, waiting for him to come home.

He washed his face and fixed his hair then went to join his family for dinner. His brother, Ben, sat quietly the whole time, and Levi wondered again what it was that always had his brother in such a shitty mood. Ben was the oldest, and Levi was the youngest; they had never shared any interests or hobbies and hadn't spent much time together. In his earliest family memories, Ben stood out as an easily irritated and unpredictable bully who liked to pinch and tease his youngest sibling. By the time Levi had gotten to high school, he'd given up on trying to be brothers with Ben and had simply avoided him.

Ruth and Naomi chatted with their mother, and Levi picked anxiously at his food. Coming home wasn't supposed to feel this weird, but he didn't usually have something to hide from his family. He wondered what else was being kept secret by the people around him.

"You're not eating," his grandmother said.

He looked up. "I am."

"Don't tell me you're watching your weight."

"No, Bubbe, I'm not."

"So why aren't you eating?"

He shoveled a few mouthfuls of food into his mouth, and after a few minutes, his mother said, "You know, your father and I have started doing Zumba together at the gym."

"I know, he told me."

"It's just something that might be fun for you, too."

"I don't think so, Mom."

"Your father didn't think he would like it either," she said.

"I'm fine, Mom. I ride my bike everywhere anyway, and I swim a lot."

"Mom, leave him alone," Ruth said.

"It's important to take care of your health," his mother said mildly. "It's all I'm saying."

Ruth and Naomi gave him sympathetic looks, and he smiled at them. His phone dinged again, and his mother said, "Not at the table."

He didn't answer it.

"So, um are you seeing anyone?" Naomi asked over dessert.

"Uh..."

It would have been a shitty, mean lie to say he wasn't, but Kato would never know, and he would never be able to explain anything sufficiently to his family. They would want to know facts, see a picture, about the girl he was seeing, and he didn't know how to handle that.

"I don't know, I guess, not really."

"That's not an answer," Naomi said.

He shrugged and filled his mouth so he would have an excuse not to talk. When he felt he'd sat and listened for long enough, he said, "Um, I'm really tired, is it okay if I go to bed early?"

Everyone told him to go, and once he was in his room, he lay down and checked his phone. He called Emily, and when she answered, she asked, "So how is it?"

"Fine, so far. I mean, my mom thinks I should do Zumba—"

She laughed.

"But that's about it. Well, and they think you're my girlfriend."

She laughed harder at the idea.

"Hey, all right, calm down," she said to someone on the other end. "He wants to talk to you."

"Okay."

He heard her hand over the phone, and then, faintly, he heard her say, "No, the other way."

A moment later, Kato said, "Hello?"

"Hi." He smiled.

"Levi?"

"Yeah. It's me."

"Is...it's weird. Not to see you."

"You mean while we're talking or in general?"

"Both."

"How are you?"

"Okay. Um. I miss you."

"I miss you, too."

"How was the plane?"

"Fine."

"Emily showed me video. It...um. I don't know. Dangerous."

"No, people fly all the time," he said. "I'm fine."

"I know."

"How's everything?"

"Charlotte likes the pictures I made," he said.

"Of course, she does. She's going to have you going out taking pictures for the rest of your life." After he'd spoken, he was hit hard by the thought that he didn't know how long Kato would live for or even how old he was.

Through his door, Naomi called, "I thought you were going to sleep," then let herself in.

He sat up.

"Who are you talking to?"

"No one," he said.

"What?" Kato asked.

"Uh."

"Come on, who is it?" she asked.

"Levi?" Kato said.

"Nothing, sorry, it's just my sister. Um, I'll talk to you later, okay?"

"Okay." Kato didn't sound happy about it, but Levi hung up anyway.

"Why are you being so sketchy?" His sister came all the way into the room and closed the door. "What's up with you?"

"Nothing."

She leaned against his door, arms crossed. "You're acting weird."

"I'm not."

"Come on, don't bullshit me," she said.

"I'm just...you know, stressed, with school and stuff."

She pressed her lips together. "You know, I'm your sister, right, not a commie spy? You can talk to me."

He sighed.

"Come on." Naomi came to sit next to him.

All through high school, she had been his secret keeper, his ride to and from parties, the one who bought alcohol for him and his friends, who never told when he'd gotten detention or when his girlfriend was over when she wasn't supposed to be.

"You really can't tell anyone else," he said. "Not even Ruthie."

She frowned. "I won't."

"I am seeing someone."

"Okay, so what?"

"Um. Not a girl."

"What!?"

"Goddammit. Shh!"

"Levi, you went out with Melanie for *two years*."

"Oh, what? So?"

"So you were gay the whole time?" she hissed.

"No, I'm...I'm not gay." He rubbed his eyes.

She made a face.

"I'm *not*. It's just...you know, I like...people for who they are, it doesn't matter if they're a boy or a girl or anything else."

"Or anything else?" she asked.

"Yeah, or anything else." He started to feel defensive and wished he hadn't said anything.

"What, like unicorns?"

"Stop it."

She looked at him sharply, surprised by the harsh way he'd spoken. "You mean like transsexual people?"

He shrugged. It wasn't exactly what he'd meant, but it wasn't wholly wrong, either. Maybe he should have Charlotte make "coming out" note cards for him because for him to fully come out, he didn't have to just say he liked boys, he had to deconstruct the gender binary for people.

"I guess so."

"Is that who you're seeing? A transsexual?"

"I think you're supposed to say transgender, and I don't think you're supposed to say it like it's a noun."

"What?"

"Like, not he's a transsexual. He's a transgender man," he said.

"Are you dating...uh, someone like that?"

"No," he said. "He's just a guy."

"Oh."

They sat together quietly for a while, until he said, "Really, promise you won't tell anyone."

"I won't."

"Promise."

"I promise. Really."

He put his face in his hands.

"Um, Levi...you know. It's, uh... you're still my brother," she said. "It doesn't matter who you like."

"Thanks." He didn't feel any better. He wished she hadn't said it didn't matter because it did. It mattered because he needed acceptance, not a brush off.

She rubbed his back. "You should get some sleep, though. Flying sucks."

He nodded.

"Night."

"Night," he said.

He didn't sleep well, his body in the wrong time zone. He had faith Naomi wouldn't tell anyone; she had never tattled for drinking or for having Melanie over when his parents weren't home.

Three days later, Emily picked him up from the airport and asked, "Oh my God, what happened?"

"Um." He rubbed his face. "I ruined Rosh Hashanah."

"What?"

"I mean, not all of it, just the last day. I made my bubbe cry."

"Levi, what happened?"

"Um...I told my sister I wasn't straight, and she...told everyone."

Emily hugged him right away. "Oh my God, I'm so sorry."

He hugged her back. "It's okay."

"No, it's not okay," she said firmly.

"So, uh, I don't think I'm gonna go home for the next holiday," he said.

She held his hand on the way to the car. "Do you want to talk about it?"

He shrugged. "I don't know. It wasn't...like no one yelled or anything. It's just...Bubbe cried, and she said she wasn't mad, just that she was so surprised. I don't know. And they kept asking me questions...and Ben was a fucking dick about it."

"I'm sorry," she said. "I really am."

He shook his head. "It'll be okay, I think. I just need time."

She squeezed his hand, and once they'd been driving for a while, she said, "He really missed you."

"I feel bad he doesn't have anything to do all day."

"He's learning to read," she said. "Then he can, you know, read."

He chuckled. "Is that what that's called?"

She smiled.

When they got home, Charlotte waved to him and asked how his trip was. He shrugged. Emily offered to take his backpack, and once he'd handed it over, he headed for the beach.

Kato appeared immediately, scooting up into the sand. Levi knelt next to him, and Kato hugged him tight, pulling him so they almost toppled over.

"Hi," Levi said.

"Hi." Kato smiled at him. "You stay home now? For a long time, right?"

He nodded. "Yeah."

The creature frowned at him after a moment, his head tilted to the side. "What's wrong?"

He sat down. "Um. I don't want to talk about it right now."

Kato clicked, and Levi knew it was pensive, a little concerned, though he wasn't entirely sure what it meant. Kato touched his face. "Okay."

"What did you learn while I was gone?"

"Stars," he said. "And...the things that live deep in the sea. I can't go as deep...and I don't like that they live there. That I didn't know."

"Must be scary."

Kato nodded. "And I learned...um." He stopped to think. "There's a show about how to making things."

"I know the one you mean. I like it."

"Me too. Took pictures for Charlotte."

"Are there a lot of those pillars?"

"They're not all the same, but there are..." He counted on his fingers, whispering the numbers to himself. "Maybe...ten, near here."

Levi nodded. "Has she been interrogating you?"

"Interrogate?"

"Asking a lot of questions."

"Yes. But, I like it. It's like...being with children." He smiled, a far-off smile that said he was lost in memories, thinking about the kids he had worked with.

Levi reached out for his hand. "I. Uh."

Kato shook his head. "Don't say it."

"Say what?"

"Don't say I could find new family."

Levi sighed.

"Tired?"

He nodded.

"Get a blanket. We can nap."

Levi went, got a blanket and a snack, he spread the blanket over the sand, and Kato pulled himself up to sit by him.

They sat on the beach together for a while, talking about nothing in particular and picking at their snack until Levi said, "Hey, um, so dolphins and stuff, they need to stay wet."

"What?"

"Or they'll die, I think," he said.

"Oh."

"Well, do you need to stay wet?"

"I'm not wet now," he said.

"I mean..." He sighed. "Never mind."

"No, tell me," Kato insisted.

"I was just wondering."

Kato made a face but didn't press the issue.

"Lay down," he said, and when Levi did, he wrapped his tail around one leg and put his head on Levi's chest.

"Isn't that uncomfortable?" Levi peeked down at him.

"What?"

"You're all twisted up. Doesn't it hurt?"

"No."

Levi closed his eyes again. They lay together on the sand for a long time, talking about nothing in particular, though Levi couldn't keep his thoughts from going back to the last dinner he'd had with his family.

No one had yelled or told him to get out, but no one had smiled or told him it was okay. They hadn't told him he was bad or wrong, but they had asked if he was sure, or if this wasn't just a phase. Ben had scoffed, "Figures," and Levi still didn't know what he meant. The only comfort he had was that, as she'd kissed him goodbye, his grandmother had patted his face and said, "You be good."

He'd promised, "I will, Bubbe."

"I know, you always are," she'd said, and she had smiled at him.

It hadn't been bad. He had to be thankful it hadn't been bad. He'd heard horror stories; Charlotte's father still didn't talk to her, and he'd known for years. People had gotten kicked out, they'd gotten hit and sent to camps; people had gotten killed.

He sighed.

"What?" Kato asked.

"Nothing. I'm just glad I'm home."

"I am glad, too."

Levi spent all day on the beach, except to get food and take bathroom breaks. Emily and Charlotte came down to have dinner with them, and it seemed like they were living in an idyllic Bizarro world where two lesbians and a Jewish kid could sit down for a nice dinner with a mythical creature.

Levi resumed classes, and their daily pattern continued. He got used to his haircut, and when it started to grow in, he went back to the same woman and asked her to do what she had done before. Charlotte had Kato gather dozens of pictures for her and spent a lot of time on her computer, staring at them, trying to find a point of comparison between the runes on the whalebone pillar and a human writing system.

One day, when he came back from class, Levi went down to the beach with his backpack. He would do his homework there, and Kato would find something to do on the iPad. They would have lunch, maybe watch something together or maybe just make out.

They did that a lot, and for Levi, it was weird to have someone who touched his body eagerly, who liked the softness around his belly and thighs, who played with his chest hair and left kisses on his fingertips.

He found Kato on his usual rock, his tail curled up and not dangling in the water. He was staring at the iPad with an intense fascination, but when Levi approached, he looked up and stopped whatever video he had been watching.

He looked nervous, which Levi found very odd.

"What were you doing?"

"Nothing."

"Did you just lie to me?" Levi asked, because, to his knowledge, it had never happened before.

"No."

Levi sat next to Kato and tried to look at the iPad, but the creature held it close to his chest.

"What were you watching?"

"Nothing."

"Kato." He began to feel concerned.

"I wasn't."

Levi reached out his hand for the iPad, and Kato wouldn't give it to him.

"Come on."

"*No.*"

Levi took his hand back, frowning, feeling disoriented. "Okay. Sorry. I just...you know, I don't know, you can tell me anything."

He pulled his backpack onto his lap and rummaged through it, not sure what he was looking for but knowing he had an assigned reading or something to do in there. Kato fidgeted, glancing at him now and again, the tablet still held close to him.

They were quiet while Levi pulled out the article he was supposed to read, and though he tried to focus, he couldn't. He thought maybe he should leave Kato alone and go back up to the house and then couldn't get the idea out of his head.

He glanced up from his article to find Kato looking at him. "Uh, did you want to be alone?"

"No."

"Okay."

After another few minutes, Kato said, "I...I know how we are...in the sea. I understand the way things should be...the right way to act."

Levi looked up.

"But I don't understand...what to do here. With us. I..." He sighed and said something that Levi understood to be an expression of frustration.

"It's okay. Take your time." Levi set aside his highlighter and article, turning to face Kato. "What's up?"

Kato glanced down at the iPad he had cradled in his lap and handed it over to Levi. "I was...I wondered about, how..."

Levi looked at the webpage Kato had been hiding from him before and found the scene the video was paused on so explicit he had to laugh. Kato had found a porn site and had been watching a muscle-bound man plow a brunette with high socks and pigtails.

Kato shook his head. "I don't...um."

Levi grinned. "Oh my god, you're such a dork."

"I know how to do with others like me, but with you...I don't know what's right, I don't know what's...too early. Too much. Not okay."

"You could have asked me," Levi said.

Kato shook his head.

"Why not?"

"You said you have not done much. You get...nervous about things. I didn't want to make you scared."

Levi couldn't stop smiling, feeling a little giddy. He set aside the iPad and pulled Kato into his arms.

"You're such a dork, thank you."

He held him tight, and Kato hugged him back but pulled away after a moment.

"I still...I still don't know."

"Well, what did you Google?"

"Sex."

Levi laughed.

"But, um, this one...I don't like it. It's..." He searched for the right word but then just shook his head.

"Yeah, it gets...pretty brutal, some of the stuff out there," Levi agreed, looking down at the paused video. "But um, you know, porn isn't really what sex is like. It's...you know, it's staged. Besides, you don't like girls."

Kato shrugged. "I couldn't find any without girls."

Levi debated for a moment then clicked the search bar and typed in a website he knew wouldn't be too horrifying with slightly more authentic videos. He handed the tablet back over, and Kato glanced at him uncertainly.

"It's, uh...this one is all guys," Levi said. "I can go if you want."

Kato's face scrunched: the face he made when he didn't understand something, when he had to think hard about what was happening.

Finally, he said, "You can stay."

Levi nodded.

Kato scrolled through the videos and clicked on one where the set up was "new roommates in college".

It occurred to Levi it might be odd, showing porn to Kato, watching it with him, but tried not to think about too much. Halfway through, Kato paused the video again and looked at Levi, worried.

"What?"

"Um...it's big."

Levi laughed again.

"I'm not...mine is...not like that," Kato said, looking back at over-large penis sported by the man on screen.

"I know, I've seen it, remember?" he said. "I told you, porn isn't what real sex is like. I don't have abs or a huge dick either. It's just...it's a business, making these videos, and they try to make them the way people think it should be not the way it is. So they make the people look a certain way, and they make the sex look a certain way."

Kato nodded.

"So do you want to see the rest?"

Kato tapped the play button and stared at the video, his lips pressed tight together most of the time. He didn't seem excited by it but concerned. Levi tried to figure out what could be worrying Kato, which helped him not get too excited about the video.

When it was over, Kato set aside the iPad, and Levi asked, "What's wrong?"

Kato shook his head. "It's different."

"Don't get all pouty about one video," Levi said. "What's really wrong?"

"You...you get scared of new things, and you said you hadn't done much sex before and I don't want you to be scared."

"I've had sex before," Levi said. "Just not with a guy. You don't have to worry about scaring me."

Kato sighed again, and Levi took his hand. He still hadn't figured out the right way to hold hands with webbed fingers, but he was working on it.

"Listen, if you're so worried, we just won't have sex," Levi joked.

Kato nodded sagely.

"Kato, I was kidding. This isn't like you, what's going on?"

"I don't know. I feel not right. I feel sad. All the time." The quiet confession unsettled Levi.

"Come on." Levi stood.

"Where?" Kato asked and squawked when Levi picked him up, slipping an arm around his torso and one under his tail. "What are you doing?"

"Stop wiggling! You're heavy!"

"What are you doing?"

"I'm gonna take you inside."

"What?"

"Yeah, come on. Hold on to me," Levi said.

Kato held tight to him, his tail trailing on the sand as Levi carried him up to the house.

"Knock on the door for me," Levi said once they'd gotten to the doorstep.

Kato knocked on the door, and Emily answered, frowning at first, then her eyes going wide.

"Levi, what are you doing!?"

"Showing him the house," he said, pushing through the door.

Kato stared at everything and pointed to the couch in the living room.

"Couch," he said.

"Yup."

"Like...on the shows. You sit there."

Levi grinned. "Yeah, you do. Do you want to sit on the couch?"

Kato nodded eagerly. Levi brought him over and helped him settle into the couch. He kept running his hands over the fabric, pushing into the cushions.

From the kitchen, Emily and Charlotte watched.

"He's not wet, is he?" Charlotte asked, "'Cause otherwise the couch is gonna be wet."

"He's fine," Levi said.

For nearly an hour, he showed Kato all the things in the house, things he had seen only in shows and movies. He watched, fascinated, as Charlotte made brownies and laughed like a child when he got to turn on the faucet in the bathroom and flush the toilet.

After he'd played with the shower, he looked up at Levi from the bathtub and said, "Bed?"

"What, are you tired?"

He shook his head. "No, I want to see a bed."

Levi handed him a towel, and he gingerly patted the water off his skin, looking uncomfortable the whole time. When he was mostly dry, Levi brought him to his bedroom, kicking his pile of dirty clothes out of the way. He deposited Kato on the bed and sat beside him.

"Your bed?" Kato asked.

"Well, it'd be weird to take you to Emily's room," he said.

Kato rolled over onto his stomach to be close to the edge and reached over to touch all the things on the bedside table. After he had touched each one, he rolled onto his back and looked up onto the ceiling. His tail hung off the side of the bed and touched the floor.

"You sleep here?"

"Yes."

"It's soft."

"Sure."

Kato took his hand and pulled him down onto the mattress. He pointed to the ceiling fan. "What's that?"

"A fan. Makes the air move around when it's hot, makes it breezy."

The creature nodded. He took one of the pillows and clutched it to his chest.

"Are you still sad?"

"No."

"Good. I'm sorry this is tough on you," Levi said. "I want to help, if I can, so you should tell me when you're sad."

Someone knocked on the door, and Charlotte asked, "Uh, are you guys doing something? 'Cause the brownies are done, so I brought you some but if you're busy, I can go."

"You can come in," Levi said, and she handed over the brownies. "Thanks."

"Yeah, no problem. I don't even like them, I just like to bake."

"You'll make a man very happy someday."

She frowned. "I didn't not understand it," she clarified, "It's just not funny."

"I'm sorry," he said. "I'm surprised, though, my people are notoriously funny."

"Yeah, well, I don't like Woody Allen either."

"Shit, well, I'm not a child rapist, so let's not make too many comparisons," he said. "Thanks for the brownies."

"You're welcome," she said and left.

Levi rested the plate on his stomach and sat up a little. He picked a piece off the brownie and ate it, then glanced at Kato, who hadn't taken anything and was looking at him.

"What?" he asked.

Kato shook his head.

"Try it. It's chocolate," he said. "You like chocolate."

"I know."

"Quit looking at me."

"Why?"

"I don't know. It's weirding me out." Levi was unused to the uninterrupted gaze of another; he was not the type of guy who would be longingly stared after.

Kato smiled. "I like you."

"Yeah, I like you too," Levi said. "Seriously, I'm not gonna eat both of these by myself. Come on."

Kato took a piece of it then made a face.

"What?"

He rubbed his fingers together. "It's...soft."

"Yeah, it's supposed to be."

"Not what I, um...thought would be."

"Do you like it?"

"I don't know."

Levi smiled.

A little while later, they went back down to the beach, and Kato swam around while Levi did his homework.

Before September was over, Levi got a phone call. The phone jangled while he had his head bent over a textbook, trying to make himself memorize the difference between the French and English Enlightenment. Kato looked up when the phone rang then tugged on Levi's sleeve.

"What?" he asked.

"Phone."

"Oh. Right." Levi looked at it and saw the call was from his grandmother. He instantly thought of all the bad things that could have happened. He answered, "Bubbe?"

"Why do you sound so sad?"

"Nothing...just wasn't expecting you to call."

"Oh, well...you know. I wanted to talk. How've you been doing? Have you been eating? Don't let what your mother said get to you. She was always so tiny. She doesn't understand. You're just like your grandfather, you know, he was so tall."

"Is that what you wanted to talk about?" The topic very well could have been eating away at her for days.

"No, I just wanted to let you know I've been thinking about you. After what your sister told us...well, I just wasn't expecting it. I was so shocked."

"I'm sorry, Bubbe."

"The look you had on your face, you looked so...my goodness, I hate seeing you look like so upset. I didn't know what to do, but I've been talking with Rabbi Schultz—"

"Bubbe!"

"And he's such a nice man, so understanding, you know, and we talked for a long time, so I wanted to call and let you know I'm here for you."

"What?"

"I'm old, I'm not stupid, and I know what can happen to boys who get involved with things like this. I mean, personally, I never saw so much of a problem with it, but you know, I never expected! I never knew any, though I always suspected Mabel and Clara weren't really cousins. Anyways, is he a nice boy?"

"Um. Yeah."

"What's his name? What's he like? Is he handsome? What does he do for work? Is he in school, too?" she asked.

"Um."

"What, you don't know his name?"

"No, his name is Kato."

"That's different."

"Yeah, he's uh...he's not from here, you know."

"Well, no, I don't know," she said.

Kato, at the sound of his name, had sat up again and was looking at Levi. He tugged on his sleeve.

"But is it serious?"

"I don't know," he said. "I hope...you know, I hope so. But he's...like I said, he's not from around here. I don't know if he'll be able to stay."

"A terrible thing. It happened to your Aunt Esther. She was so broken up for months."

"Yeah."

"So what does he do?"

"He's a teacher. Um. History."

"Education is very important."

Kato was staring him down, and Levi was struck with an idea. "Do you want to talk to him?"

"Right now? I don't see why not, go ahead."

Levi handed the phone over to Kato and said, "It's my grandmother."

Kato stared.

"Then next time mind your own business," he said and put the phone to Kato's ear.

"Uh...Hi?" Kato said.

Levi could hear his grandmother talking on the other end and grinned. She talked for about three minutes before Kato could say something else. She must have asked him a question because he answered with a hesitant, "No?"

After about ten minutes, Kato handed back the phone and said, "She says give the phone back to you."

Levi grinned and said, "Hi."

"He's certainly got a very different accent. I've never heard anyone like it before. Sounds nice, though, are we going to get to meet him?"

"I don't know."

"Anyway, I have to go for lunch with your aunt in a little while, and I need to fix my hair. I love you."

"I love you, too," he said. He put his phone aside.

Kato pushed him.

"What?"

"What is Jewish? Who is...Root and Nami and Benanmin and Sarah? What is Rash-ash-na, and you didn't *tell* me you had fight with your family!"

Levi stared. "It wasn't a fight. Um. You know, not really. Ruth, Naomi, and Benjamin are my brother and sisters, Sarah is my mother. Rosh Hashanah is the holiday I went home for, and Jewish is my religion."

"Your family fought about me?"

"No, it wasn't...it's just, I told Naomi I was seeing someone and asked her not to tell, but she told everyone else."

"Why did you ask her not tell? Because...I'm not the same?"

"Kato, it's...it's kind of complicated."

"So tell me."

"My family didn't know that I was into guys," he said.

Kato frowned and shook his head after a few moment of contemplation. "Lost me."

"It's just, um, well, some people don't think it's okay for two guys, or two girls, to be together."

Kato's frown deepened.

"It's just...it's hard to explain. So my family didn't know. And I wasn't going to tell them."

"You told them that I'm..." He thought, put a hand to his chest. "Not a human?"

"No. I didn't. We didn't really talk about you," he said and saw that Kato looked upset. "It's not because you're not important to me, it's just...you know, in some places it's illegal...you know, there are laws against gay marriage. I can't even imagine what they'd do about us!"

"Marriage."

"Yeah, it's—"

"I know what it is. I watched all those movies," he said, and Levi knew he was referring to the Disney movies they'd watched together.

"Kato, I told you it was complicated."

"I know."

Levi took his hand and scooted closer to him. "It's not what I'm worried about right now. Right now I just want to spend time with you, okay?"

"Okay."

"So you're not mad?"

"No."

Levi leaned over and kissed his cheek. "Good."

"Work tomorrow?" he asked.

"No."

"School tomorrow?"

"No."

Kato smiled. "Come swim."

"Can I finish this first?"

Kato shook his head. "No. Take a break."

"Okay." He set aside his book and notes, shoving them into his backpack. He put aside his phone and shirt, and Kato tugged on his shorts.

"I don't know," he said.

Kato nodded.

"Maybe once we're in the water," he said. He had not been naked around Kato again, not since the first time he'd been goaded into it. He waded into the water, and Kato circled around him once then swam away.

It was utterly alien to see him swim; it reminded Levi that he was not human, more than his sharp teeth or black eyes, more than being hairless with webbed fingers and a tail. Watching him move through the sea made Kato seem entirely different than the helpless, stranded thing he became on land.

Kato came back and took his hand, pulling him in deeper. Levi allowed himself to be pulled, and he let Kato cradle him.

They looked up at the sky together, and Kato pointed to one of the clouds and said something Levi didn't understand. Levi looked at the cloud and guessed, "An octopus?"

"Lots of tails?"

"Yeah."

"Oc-to-pus."

"The one to the left looks like a seagull."

Kato chirped his agreement. He tightened his tail around Levi and scooted him up a little higher. For a moment, it seemed an innocent gesture of affection until his fingers tugged at the strings of Levi's bathing suit.

For a moment, Levi didn't know what to do. If he said stop, Kato would, and he knew it; a very large part of him wanted to say it. The same part of him that had been afraid to even admit he was attracted to the creature.

Kato kissed Levi's throat, and Levi's heart quickened. His fingers skimmed along the waistband, tickling almost, then slid inside.

"Um," Levi said softly, and Kato pulled his hand back. "Let go of me for a second."

Kato released him carefully and sunk into the water so he was only visible from the eyes up. He watched as Levi fumbled in the water then tossed his suit onto one of the nearby rocks.

"Um," Levi said again because he had no idea what else to say. He had never been good at this. Kato waited, watching. "You can, um, you can come hold me again if you want."

Kato came over and embraced him, cooing contentedly. He kissed Levi and touched his face, then wrapped himself around him again, this time so they were face to face. Levi was never sure how they managed to stay afloat at moments like these but couldn't think about it for long with their bodies so close together.

Kato's hands roamed between Levi's legs and carefully touched what he found there. At times, he seemed almost more curious than excited until Levi got hard, and Kato smiled at him, kissing his shoulder and making quiet, satisfied noises Levi thought might have been dirty talk.

It was hard to think straight like this, to make anything that could have counted as a good choice. Kato ran one hand down his back, and it sent an alarm through Levi. He didn't think he was ready to go that far, not now, not like this.

"Um," he said.

Kato took his hand back, kissing him again. "Is this good?" He was still holding him gently between the legs, giving a stroke or a little squeeze now and again.

"Yes, just..." He didn't want him to stop, he knew that much. The slow touches started to make Levi desperate for something more, and he thrust, unthinking.

"Please," Levi said.

"Tell me what you want."

"I want you to keep touching me like you are, please."

Kato kissed him again and moved his hand faster, pushing his own erection against Levi. It sent a ripple through Levi, and he reached out to touch Kato too.

"Do you want to try something?" Kato asked.

"Um, what?"

"To put yours in me."

He hadn't expected the offer. He hadn't had any idea where this encounter was going. "Yes," Levi said immediately, too eager but Kato grinned.

"Are you ready?"

Levi nodded.

Kato pushed himself closer, putting Levi just below where his own penis protruded, rubbing himself with Levi's head.

"Here," he said, "But not too fast."

Levi nodded, glad to know at least that much was the same between their species. He pushed in slowly, carefully, and continued to stroke Kato at the same time.

He made a sound Levi had never heard before.

"Was that...good?" Levi asked.

"Yes."

Kato made a lot of noises for the next few minutes that Levi had never heard, but from the way he writhed and clung to Levi, he seemed to be enjoying himself. They came about a minute apart, Levi first and Kato after.

Levi was out of breath, and when Kato released him, he couldn't manage to tread water very well. Screwing in the water had made him use muscles he didn't know he could, and coming like that had left him lightheaded.

Kato took his hand and pulled him to the sand, where he lay down and arranged Levi next to him, twining his tail around his hips and thighs and putting Levi's head on his outstretched arm.

"See, not very bad," Kato said, half-smiling.

Levi laughed and nestled closer to him. "No. It was good. Emily's never gonna let me hear the end of this."

Kato didn't say anything and Levi wondered if the unreality of what they had done was sinking in for him, too. It had been unplanned, unprotected and, now that the need of the moment had faded, the whole thing felt like a dream.

He wondered if mythic sea creatures had STDs. It would have been good to ask beforehand and now it felt too late.

"Hey. Can I ask you something?"

"Okay."

"How come you can float?"

"I don't know."

"I mean, just...you hold me up. Shouldn't we be too heavy?"

Kato made a face. "Doesn't matter." This was apparently not his idea of worthwhile pillow talk.

"I'm just curious."

"Ask me something different," Kato said.

"Like what?"

"Something I can tell to you."

Levi thought for a minute. "Have you been with a lot of people?"

Kato considered the question and then shrugged. "I don't know. What's a lot?"

Levi had no definition for what a lot of people would be and realized it was a useless question. "Do you like it better the way we did it or if you were the one...um...being inside of me?"

"Doesn't matter. Both good."

"It doesn't hurt your tail to curl up like this?"

"I told you it doesn't."

"It looks like it hurts."

"No."

"Why do you speak English so good?" Levi asked. "It's ridiculous, you know. I spent years at Hebrew school! How can you learn so fast?"

Kato shrugged. "I don't know."

"You're really smart, aren't you? You must sit there all the time and listen to us and think we're so stupid."

"No. Not stupid," Kato reassured.

"My grandfather was like that, you know. He was a lawyer in Poland, but they moved here, and he couldn't really get ahold of English. So he worked his whole life here as a janitor, and he couldn't really talk to us. It must have driven him crazy, I bet, to have had so many thoughts, you know, stuck in his head," Levi said.

Kato listened and looked at him, his mouth half-curved into a smile.

"Why do you always look at me like that?"

"I like to look at you," Kato said. "You like to look at me?"

"Yes," Levi said, "But you're beautiful."

"You're fat." He said it the same way Levi had said beautiful, with a smile and with reverence. "Soft. You have, uh." He made a twisting motion with his finger. "Curly. You have curly hair. Your eyes..."

"My eyes are just brown," Levi said.

"Brown is good," Kato said.

So many people had brown eyes. Levi wondered if Kato would like other men better if he had the chance to meet them.

"Can I ask you something?"

"Only if I know the answer."

"Why did you...I mean, at first...why did you like me?"

"Because you helped me. You showed me fishing. You shared with me," he said then added, "But...also because I like to touch you. There is something...I don't know. Why are your questions always so hard? There is something good about the way I feel when I touch you."

"Come on, you worked with kids, you must be used to questions."

"Babies ask different questions. They ask what are those things in the sky, what is that loud thing that goes so fast, why do sharks come when there's blood, why is Manit so big." He smiled to himself.

"You miss them."

"I love them. Their whole lives I know them."

"I know you think it's a bad idea, but maybe you should try to go back. Maybe they won't let you stay, but maybe you could visit. Or at least be able to say goodbye," Levi said. "I would go with you, you know, in case something went wrong...but it can't hurt to try."

Kato looked at him for a while, contemplative. "Maybe."

Levi kissed him. "Let me know."

Charlotte and Levi sat together watching Emily and Kato take selfies on her phone. Kato had watched her take one and had immediately wanted a picture of himself. He had nearly dropped the phone in surprise when he'd seen the picture she'd taken.

Kato had touched the screen gingerly. "Is that me?"

"No, it's the other mermaid living on my beach," had been Emily's answer.

Charlotte held out a bag of gummy bears to Levi, and Levi picked out a red one.

"They're pretty cute," Charlotte said.

Levi smiled. "I know."

"I mean, we're doing all right for ourselves, really," Charlotte said, "Considering what we're working with."

Levi glanced at her. "You're all right, you know."

She wrinkled her nose. "You don't have to be nice."

"No, I mean it," he said.

She didn't look like she believed him, but she didn't argue. Like him, and unlike Emily, she hadn't fit in as a kid. She was different, in manner and appearance, from most people and her differentness must have gotten her teased, if not outright bullied. He took another gummy bear without saying anything else.

"Big plans for Halloween?" Levi asked after a few minutes. His phone dinged, and he looked down to see Emily had texted him a series of photos.

"Yes."

"What?"

"You'll have to wait and see," she said, which she always did.

She spent a good part of September and October making a costume every year, and they always turned out fantastic. Emily would plan a party, and Charlotte would probably make a costume for her, too. She would give Levi half a dozen suggestions for what to wear, and he would never wear anything more elaborate than a tuxedo t-shirt.

Kato called his name, and Levi looked over. The creature waved him over, and he went.

"What's up?" Levi asked.

"Come here," Kato said, holding out a hand.

Levi took it hesitantly, and Emily said, "Make sure you actually smile."

"Oh, no, don't take my picture."

Kato pouted.

"Yes take your picture," he insisted. "*Our* picture."

"All right, I guess," Levi said, though he didn't want to at all. He hated pictures of himself but considered it was obligatory to have at least one picture as a couple.

Kato wrapped his arms around Levi and held him close, putting his lips to Levi's cheek. Emily made an "aw" noise and took a picture, but she didn't stop at one. She took several and then sent them to Levi's phone after they had met both of their approval.

"Come in," Kato said, looking at the water. To Emily, he said, "You, too."

"You sure?" she asked.

He nodded and said, "Yes," in a way that sounded like he didn't know why she wouldn't.

"You don't want to be alone?" she asked.

He narrowed his eyes and thought for a moment then shook his head. "No."

Levi had already taken to the water, floating on his back and waiting.

"Charlotte?" Kato asked Emily.

"Um, no, she's...you know, got girl stuff going on," Emily said, shedding most of her clothing and wading in.

Kato pushed himself off the sand and into the waves. "What's girl stuff?"

"You know."

"I think if mermaids got periods, they'd be shark-bait," Levi said.

"Oh, right," Emily said. "Um, I'll tell you about it later."

"Okay." Kato reached out to take her hand and grasped it lightly, pulling her along as they swam.

After about an hour, Emily excused herself, saying she needed something to drink and asked them what they wanted. She headed up to the house, and Kato watched her go, asking, "What's a girl problem?"

"She said she'd tell you later," Levi said. "Besides, I'm not a girl."

Kato huffed a little, and Levi could have explained things to him but wasn't fully comfortable with the idea. He had lived his life surrounded by women and knew enough to be sympathetic and to never ask if their period was putting them in a mood, but other than that, he liked the details to be vague.

"What do you want for dinner?" Levi asked to distract him.

It worked because Kato immediately put on his thinking face until he started to look around, concerned and listening carefully.

"It's just a speedboat or something," Levi assured. Every so often, boats or jet skis would cruise by the entrance to the beach but never turned into the small bay unless they were lost.

"I know." He sank lower in the water, up to his mouth.

"Hey."

"Boats are dangerous," he said.

"Yeah, but they're out there, and we're in here," he said. "It's a private beach, and there're signs posted not to come in."

Kato didn't look comforted, sinking in up to his eyes, and Levi took his hand. He wondered, stomach uneasy, if Kato's people had problems with boat propellers the same way dolphins and manatees did.

The sound of the speedboat grew and continued to get louder instead of fading like it normally did when boats passed by. They were floating together yards from the shore, closer to the entrance to the cove than to the sand.

Kato continued to glance around, agitated and twitchy.

Levi said, "Maybe we should go in."

The boat had gotten much louder, and Levi thought he heard more than one. Maybe they were jet skis; maybe it was just some frat boy assholes horsing around. Probably drunk.

Kato's grip tightened on his hand, and he started to swim for shore, but before they'd made it halfway, a trio of small boats ripped through the entrance to their beach. Quick as lightning, one cut them off, and the other two flanked them.

Things happened faster than Levi could follow, though it didn't help that one of the people on the boat nearest to him had jabbed him in the chest with a long pole, knocking all the air out of his lungs and sending him underwater.

When he surfaced, he saw Kato wrapped in a net, thrashing wildly and being pulled into one of the boats with a gaff.

He reached out to grab him, to pull him back, but he was struck again with the long pole. It didn't knock him under this time, and he lunged as best he could, grabbing on to one corner of the net and pulling with all his strength.

The boat titled, and Kato managed to free one hand, grabbing onto Levi's arm, his fingers digging in with their stubby nails, scraping his skin.

"Don't let go," Levi said, wrapping both his hands around Kato's arm. He pulled and got hit again for it, this time in the face. His world faded, his vision going fuzzy at the edges, his breath short, like he had stood up too fast.

One of the boats had edged closer, and one of the people pulled him; he could barely hold on, and Kato's arm slipped from his grasp. Levi heard screaming, though he wasn't sure if it was him, Kato, or one of the girls. Broad, thick hands pushed him underwater again, and when he surfaced, the boat with the entangled and writhing creature had zipped away to the exit, the other two in its wake.

He watched, not knowing what else to do, and by the time he had his thoughts back, Charlotte had come out into the water and grabbed his arm, saying, "Levi, come on. Come back in."

He let her guide him for a moment then pulled away. "We have to go after him."

"How?" she asked.

She pulled at him again, and he realized she had come in after him with all her clothes on, even her sweater. She brought him back to shore, where Emily, with makeup running down her face, was on the phone with the police, reporting what had happened with half-sentences and sobs.

Levi watched as Charlotte dried her hands on a towel and picked up her phone. He saw her open Facebook and felt enraged for a moment before he saw that she was posting a video to the site.

He watched her post the video on Facebook, Twitter, Tumblr and Youtube, bouncing up and down furiously and typing everything with one hand while her other one buzzed frantically in the air beside her. He should have been doing something, he knew that much, but all he could do was look around and cough. His lungs burned, his chest ached where he had been hit, and his whole head throbbed.

Twenty minutes later, two cops and an ambulance arrived. The cops spoke to him and the girls while the EMTs looked at his head, applying bandages to the cut on his temple, listening to his lungs and checking his eyes.

Emily recounted what she had seen, and Levi did, too; Charlotte said nothing, but she held out her phone and showed them the video she had taken.

The cops stared, and the EMTs crowded around.

One cop demanded, "What the fuck is that?"

"It's him," Emily said, her eyeliner smeared down her cheeks. "His name is Kato. That's who they took."

"It's not a person."

"He is a person, his name is Kato, you have to help him," she said and began again to cry.

The cops fell to debating amongst themselves for a while then one called into their police chief and spoke on the phone for a long time.

Another one put a hand on Emily's shoulder and said, "Don't worry, we'll do what we can, no matter what that thing is, all right? This is something serious."

Kato didn't know where he was, and he didn't know how long he had been there. It was dark, except for when someone came and checked on him and tossed a frozen fish into the squat, caged tank they had him in.

It smelled harsh and chemical, like the trails boats would leave behind. He heard the jangle and scrape of metal, and the lights turned on, hurting his eyes so he threw up a hand to cover them.

The pair approached, and Kato's nose twitched at the smell of fresh fish, sweet and mild, barely dead at all. He sank as low as he could into the little tank and watched them, just his eyes above the water. His stomach hurt, and he knew it had been a long time since they'd fed him.

The fish plunked into the water beside him, and he grabbed it, ripping into its flesh, not caring if he choked on bones or had scales in his teeth. He had not been hungry like this, not ever in his life. Caring for the children of others had always left him well-fed. Before he had cared for the little ones, he had been a child himself, and his parents had kept him fat and safe and warm. A bone jabbed into his gums, and he flinched but then resumed his feast a moment later.

He would have been mortified if his friends had seen him like this, but it felt like it had been long enough that they would have forgotten he ever existed. Levi would not forget him, he told himself.

The thought of Levi made him slow down. What could Levi be doing now, or Emily, or Charlotte? Were they looking for him? Had they given up? Had something happened to them as well? Were they also locked up somewhere, starving and dirty, gobbling down food like animals?

Was Levi even alive? The last thing Kato had seen of him was him in the water, being pushed and struck, his head slipping under.

He had to be alive; the thought of him dead turned Kato's stomach so he couldn't eat anymore.

The disquiet in his belly didn't go away, and he wondered if it was more than bad thoughts that had him feeling sick. He tasted the fish again and found it not exactly the way it should have been.

He released it.

The pair of humans hadn't left yet, and they always left after they'd fed him, except for the few times they had taken him out of the tank and stretched him out on the floor to take pictures of him.

His stomach began to hurt worse, and he couldn't keep his eyes open. Something wasn't right; maybe the fish had been spoiled. He grabbed onto one of the bars and looped his arm around it. He feared he would drown if he passed out in this tank, which was too small to unwind his tail all the way in any direction.

The next time his eyes opened, he was bound and moving, moving far too fast in something that jostled him and hurt his bones. He moved, and the two humans sitting next to him moved too, one putting their knee in his back, pressing him to the floor and the other jabbing him with something sharp. His eyes closed again.

The second time he woke, he was in a pool of odd-smelling water, clean and clear, but not very large or deep. He could stretch out his tail, and that was the first thing he did, stretching all his cramped muscles.

"God, what a fucking prize this is," a voice said.

Kato started and looked around. Behind him, he found a man, dressed in slacks and a button down. Kato stared at him.

On either side of this man were two more men and a woman with deep brown skin, but these three were dressed in tight black suits that covered their whole bodies.

Kato pushed himself deeper into the pool, away from them, winding his tail closer to himself, as though it could offer him protection.

The man in slacks said, "Tad, see if you can get him doing some tricks or something. Think of a name for him, huh? Make sure it's a him, anyways. Maybe we should do one of those polls on the Internet. People like those. I'll talk to PR about it and see what they think."

The one called Tad said, "Yes, sir, we'll see what we can get out of him."

The man in slacks patted Tad on the back then walked away, talking to himself.

Tad said to the other man that remained, "Can you fucking believe this shit?"

"No," the man said. This human had dark skin, too, darker than Emily's tan or the golden color of Charlotte's skin.

The woman said, "I don't know, I feel weird about this."

"And you don't feel weird about anything else going on here?" Tad asked.

"Yeah, but Jim—"

"Listen, Tess, you're still kind of new, so I'm gonna let you in on something. Everything Jim says is bullshit. If you want to get something done, work on getting yourself promoted," the other man interrupted.

"Don't be a dick, Angel," Tad said.

Angel ignored him and came closer to the pool. He knelt by the edge, and Tess warned, "Be careful, we don't know anything about him."

"It's a goddamn mermaid. What's the worst that can happen?" Angel asked.

"You know mermaids drown people, right?"

Kato watched Angel kneel next to the pool.

"Yeah, and did you see the fucking teeth on him when he was stretching?" Tad asked.

"So he bites me." Angel shrugged dismissively.

He reached into a bucket and pulled out a fish. It hung, dead and flaccid, between them, and Kato recalled what had happened last time he'd taken something from a human. Something about these people, the bucket, and the scrap of fish seemed familiar, though he knew he had never been anywhere like this before.

It was the first time in his life he couldn't smell the sea, but there was something about this he recognized. He sank into the water, not liking the way it tasted, still watching Angel, and thought, trying hard to remember, until it hit him, hard in the stomach.

During one of his first long afternoons on the beach with the iPad, waiting for Levi or Emily to come visit him, he had watched a movie which had looked like this, but he had turned it off halfway through. He had hated it, hated that anyone would make something so horrifying. He had assumed it to be made up in the same way he had assumed the movie about men who drank blood was made up.

"He's looking at you weird," Tess said.

"Well, he's probably not stupid," Tad said.

Kato moved to the other side of the tank. If the movie had been real, if the nightmare about whales being held prisoner was true, and if Kato had found himself in such a place, he didn't want the scrap of food the man offered him.

He curled around himself and closed his eyes. Maybe he would wake up and it would just be another bad dream, no different than the ones where sharks got into the protected beach, leaving nothing of his family but blood and scraps of flesh. He would wake up, and he would be home again.

The three humans talked softly about him, and when he woke again, it had gotten darker, but he was still in the pool. The humans were nowhere to be seen.

He looked around and saw nothing. His stomach hurt, but he ignored it. He instead thought of what Levi, Emily, and Charlotte might be doing. He thought the most about Levi, and it made his throat tighten; it hurt, but he couldn't stop. He didn't want to.

He floated on his back and looked up at the sky. One cloud floated there. He watched the cloud move across his field of vision.

He spent days like this, watching clouds float, ignoring the humans' attempts to feed him or speak with him. One human came and manhandled him, peering into his mouth, pressing cold things against his chest and jabbing him with thin, sharp things and taking his blood.

Maybe the movies of men who drank blood were not made up either. Kato bit this human, digging his teeth into his hand when he started to poke at things. Kato did not want to be touched by a stranger, especially not one who had stolen his blood.

On the third day, he didn't eat. Angel came up to him and looked down at him severely.

"Hey."

Kato didn't look at him.

"I know you can hear me. I don't know if you can understand me, but if you don't eat on your own, we're going to force you."

Kato looked over, and Angel frowned. With that frown, Kato knew he had betrayed himself, so with a flick of his tail, he splashed Angel and bared his teeth in the hope that maybe his attention would look like aggression instead of understanding.

He didn't want them to know anything about him.

Angel sighed and walked away. Later, they came with lots of people and held him down, trying to shove a tube down his throat. He fought, and they brought more people to hold him still, half a dozen black-clad bodies pressing down on him, all of them grunting and swearing, some of them looking pained, and one firmly saying, "Well, we can't let him starve himself."

After that, his throat ached for days, and he found bruises where their hands and knees had pressed into him. The next time Angel approached him with food, he reached out for it, but Angel didn't hand it over.

Instead, he held it higher, out of Kato's reach and said, "Up."

Kato frowned.

"Up," Angel said again.

Kato reached for it, and Angel let him take it once he'd lifted himself out of the water enough.

To himself, Angel said, "And how am I supposed to think of tricks for you? I don't even know what you can do."

He looked around and then pushed open a gate Kato had ignored. He didn't care where it went to because he knew it wouldn't bring him home. Angel walked away, past the gate, and Kato peered out to see it led to a larger pool of water.

"Come on," Angel said.

Kato eyed him. Could anything beyond the gate be worse than where he was now? He swam out, cautiously, looking around. He found the semi-circle pool beyond empty, with clear walls that showed him hundreds of chairs.

Not chairs. Seats. This was somewhere people came to watch; he'd watched a movie about baseball, and the chairs in it had been called seats.

Kato circled once around the larger pool, found it barren and uninteresting, and swam back over to Angel. He pulled himself onto the platform where Angel stood and grabbed the bucket he had set at his feet.

Angel danced back, startled, and Kato shoved a handful of meat bits into his face. If they were going to make him eat and if all he had to eat were bland, mushy scraps, he would get it over with.

He could have made himself throw up after they'd fed him. He could fight every moment of this, he realized, but he had never been strong enough to fight. He had always been good with children and good at making his friends laugh, but he had never been good at being strong. He had done what Manit had told him to do, even when he didn't like it, and before Manit had been their leader, he had done what Pi'ho had told him to do.

Angel was watching him warily, he realized. He tossed aside the bucket, and when the human went to right it, he flicked it with his tail and sent it into the water.

Angel stared at it and Kato watched him.

If he went into the water to retrieve it, Kato could follow him. He would be stronger, faster in the water. Maybe they would trade with him if he had one of theirs. Maybe if he drowned every human that came near him, they would think he wasn't worth the trouble and let him go home.

Angel edged close to the water and snatched the bucket before it sank, his eyes on Kato the whole time.

Kato didn't pounce, though he considered it.

Angel took the bucket away and looked at Kato for a while, regarding him from a distance. He walked away, muttering to himself, and came back with a few things in his arms. A ball, a few hoops. He set them down on the ground, and the ball bounced away, closer to Kato.

Angel reached for it, and Kato grabbed it, not because he wanted it, but because Angel had reached for it. The human didn't try to take it from him.

Kato held it in his arms for a moment then rolled it between his hands. It felt good to have something to hold, something to do with his hands.

After a few more minutes of watching, Angel walked away.

When he was gone, Kato lay down on the platform, his tail moving lazily in the water. He looked up at the sky, which had no clouds, then tossed the ball into the air. He caught it, barely, almost getting hit in the face.

He tossed it in the air for a while longer then into the water. He flicked it with his tail and sent it flying into the air. He tried to catch it, but he had aimed poorly and missed by a long shot. He crawled over and got the ball then tried again.

The sun moved across the sky, and Kato managed to flick the ball to himself seven times in a row before he messed up, hitting it too hard and sending it flying to his left. It rolled across the platform, and as he crawled to get it, he saw Tad had been watching him from the corner, his pale brown hair hanging in his eyes.

Tad picked up the ball and rolled it back to Kato.

He snatched it and slithered into the water, holding the ball tight in his arms. It tried to float to the surface, and the further down he went, the harder it was to hold on to.

Eventually, he let it go and watched it zoom up to the surface, fast as anything. He retrieved the ball again and tried to push it under the water. It popped back up with a splash. Pushing the ball under and watching it pop up amused him for a minute or two, but eventually it lost entertainment value as well.

He lay on his back and floated, looking up at the sky. The sun sat overhead, and it hurt his eyes to look directly at it, but he did so anyway until they squinted shut of their own volition. He wondered if he was brave enough to take in a lungful of water, but knew he wouldn't be able to do.

Tad made a noise, and Kato opened one eye, looking over. He had knocked something over or dropped it, and when Kato looked at him, he froze, halfway bent over. Kato looked at what he had dropped and hauled himself out of the water, dragging himself to get to the phone.

Tad grabbed it and took a few steps backward. Kato reached for the phone, and Tad stared at him. He waited patiently, his hand outstretched, the fingers twitching a little with anticipation.

"What? My phone?" Tad asked, incredulous.

Kato stretched his hand a little farther.

Tad handed it over.

Kato took and tried to swipe, but it asked for a password. He held up, and Tad tapped in a password; once he had access, he tapped through, looking for the place where he could make calls. He found it and tapped in three numbers, 911, which Emily had shown him, telling him to call this if something ever happened to one of them while they were swimming, or if someone came snooping around the beach again.

"Hey!" Tad said and grabbed the phone back.

Kato didn't let go, and they struggled for a second.

"What the fuck was that!" Tad demanded once he had the phone back.

Kato tried to snatch the phone again but didn't manage it. They stared at each other for a moment before Kato retreated, going back into the larger pool and going straight for the bottom. He tucked himself against the far wall and stayed for as long as he could hold his breath, then surfaced, filled his lungs and went back.

Before it began to get dark, Angel returned, and when Kato came for another lungful of air, they didn't notice him, and he lurked at the surface, watching and listening carefully. They were talking about him, about what he had done with the phone. When Angel glanced over, he ducked back under.

When they fed him again, they lured him back into the smaller pool and closed the gate behind him. He glanced it for just a moment, concerned himself with keeping down the fish they'd brought for him and then ignored them once he'd sated his hunger.

Once they left, he undid the gate himself and let himself into the larger pool. He spent the night going through all the things that had been left on the platform.

In the morning, when they came and found him not in the large or small pool, with the gate opened and things scattered around the platform, he heard them search anxiously for him. He thought about calling for help but didn't. He had spent the early morning, the hours with faint light, stuck on a piece of scenery. He had climbed up using his arms, and he hadn't found a way down because his only option seemed to be face first and that had made him shaky and dizzy when he'd tried.

They didn't see him, none of them looking up, not until they were all gathered together, swearing and shouting; he laughed, and they all looked up slowly, not believing their eyes.

"See this is what I'm talking about!" Tad said. "Something's not right about him."

"Just because dolphins don't look like us—" Tess began.

"A dolphin wouldn't know how to dial 911!" Tad cut her off.

"So clearly he's dealt with people before," she said. "He knows what we are."

"How are we going to get him down?" Angel looked up at him. "If you jump, we'll catch you."

"Don't have him jump. Do you know how much trouble we'd be in if he got hurt?" Tad said.

"All right, so we can get a blanket or something," Tess suggested.

They went off and came back a few minutes later with a tarp.

"Come on," Angel said.

Kato shook his head.

"What? Are you scared?" Angel asked.

Kato nodded.

Angel sighed, released his corner of the tarp and said to Tad, "Take up the slack."

He came over to where Kato had gotten stuck. "Come on. I'll help you down, and you can fall into the tarp."

Kato shook his head.

Angel pulled himself up closer, standing on an outcropping of the fake rock. He found a handhold and reached his free hand out to Kato.

"Come on, or we're all gonna get in trouble."

Kato considered his statement.

"What do you think they'll do if they know you can get out on your own?"

Kato took his hand and scooted over to the edge; he let the man pull him off and squeezed his eyes shut as he fell. He hit the tarp, and they set him down a moment later. He sat up, looked at them for a moment then slipped back into the larger pool.

"How are we going to get him to do anything?" Tad asked.

"I don't know. Talking to him seems to work," Tess said. "We'll find out what he wants and tell him he can have it if he does what we ask."

"But what does he want?" Angel mused.

Kato splashed them.

"Probably for us to fuck off," Tess said.

"Hey," Tad called over to him. "What do you want? You know, you want to make a deal?"

Kato thought about answering but didn't. He took up one of the balls he had thrown into the pool during the night and cradled it to his chest, floating on his back. He ignored them for the rest of the day and for the rest of the week.

The man in slacks came back several days later and looked at him for a long time.

"He doesn't do much," he pronounced.

"We've got to find a motivator," Angel said.

"Well, you better find it fast," the man advised. "Don't have a lot of time left before we're supposed to open this exhibit."

"I don't know."

"Get him looking lively at least," the man said. "Whatever you need to do. People will come see him even if he doesn't do tricks. A fucking mermaid."

"Merman," Tess said.

"Doesn't matter," the man said. "PR thinks polling to name him is a good idea."

Kato looked over, and Tad saw him looking.

"Any ideas to put up there?" the man asked.

Kato threw the ball at him, and Tad said, "Hey, watch out!"

The man didn't move fast enough and got hit in the back of the head with the ball.

"What was that?" the man asked, his face red.

"He doesn't like it when we talk about him," Tess said.

"You're telling me he understands that we're talking about him?" The man had his eyebrows raised and a lot of sneer in his tone.

"I'm pretty sure," she said.

"For a diversity hire, you're not too stupid," the man told her.

Her face contorted, and Kato eyed the way her hands balled at her sides.

"Anyway, figure something out," the man in slacks said and walked away.

Once he was gone, Tess launched into a tirade Kato couldn't follow. Without noticing, he had drifted closer to them, trying to listen in and comprehend what she was saying. Angel responded, and Kato couldn't understand him either.

He gasped to himself when he realized they were speaking another language, and they looked over at him.

"He gives me the creeps," Tad said.

Kato gave him the finger.

"See!" Tad cried.

"So what's your name, anyway?" Angel asked.

Kato almost answered, his mouth half-opened before he decided not to respond.

"My name's Angel," he said.

Kato frowned at him.

Angel came over to sit at the edge of the platform, his legs in the water. None of them had ever come close, let alone in, the water while Kato was swimming. He held out his hand and said, "We can work together, you know."

Kato snaked out his tail and wrapped it around Angel's ankle, pulling him into the water. Tess screamed, covering her mouth, and Tad jumped back. Kato held him for only a minute, dragging him deeper into the pool, farther from the platform.

Once released, Angel surfaced, coughing.

Kato circled around him, not too close but not far enough away that the human could escape. Angel treaded water, watching him, coughing every so often. He seemed calm, but Kato felt his heartbeats through the water. Kato moved a little closer, and Angel flinched; Kato smiled.

"I know what happened to you," Angel said.

Kato slowed then stopped.

"I know they took you from somewhere. There's no way you were born in captivity, you used to be in the ocean somewhere. I know you have a family or something out there, but they're not going to let you go." When he spoke, he held Kato's gaze, his eyes the flat, deep green of the sea in places where plants grew. "They're gonna milk every last dime they can get out of you. The most I can do for you is make it better while they do."

"Angel?" Tess called.

He didn't answer her.

"Let me help you," he said.

"I want to go home," Kato said.

Angel stared at him for a moment then came back to his senses. "I can't get you there."

"Then I don't need you to help me," Kato said.

"He fucking talks!" Tess screeched.

Kato made a face at her then swam away from Angel, who paddled back to the platform.

Five days later, Tess came and stood at the edge of the platform and looked down into the pool. From his spot on the wall, Kato could see her, and he thought about swimming up to grab her. Instead, he released the ball he'd been holding and smiled to himself when she jumped back.

He followed the ball up, more slowly, to get some air and to see if it was time to eat yet. They had tried a few times to get him to do something in exchange for food, and he had bitten Tad on the calf, hard enough to draw blood. He still walked with a limp.

When he surfaced, she looked at him and asked, "Want to know your name?"

He stared at her, eyes narrowed, not sure what she meant.

"The Internet voted. Pretty soon people are going to come see Qalupalik."

He wrinkled his nose.

"They haven't announced it yet, but it's the name with the most votes. I was hoping for Charlie," she said. "So what do you think? Do you like it?"

He shook his head. He didn't like it, not at all.

"So what's your real name?" she asked. "I mean, we've got to call you something."

"Kato."

"What?"

"Kay-toe," he said more slowly.

"Kato, all right," she said. "Soon people are going to come see you, Kato, and take your picture."

He shrugged. He swam a little closer to her, trying to look like he was drifting over instead of doing it on purpose. He spent all day avoiding these humans because he wanted badly to talk to them. He wanted to touch their skin, to have anything to hold close.

"So are you going to entertain them?" she asked.

He shook his head.

"I think if you did, if you played along," she said, "I think...if we make it seem like you talking is a trick, then maybe..." She trailed off.

"Maybe what?" he asked.

"You're gonna be on the news," she said. "You're gonna be famous."

He nodded.

"So you have a voice."

"And?"

"And the dolphins don't. The whales can't talk," she said. "But if you said something, people would know."

He had ended up right next to her without meaning to do so. "If I said something..."

"Yeah," she said. "I think it would help."

He put his hand on hers, not thinking about it, and she pulled back. It was a fair reaction, he realized; he had been terrorizing them.

"What tricks?"

She squinted out into the stands for a moment. "I don't know. What can you do?"

"Uh...swim? Catch fish. Tell history."

"What do you mean?"

"To the little ones, I told our history."

"Really?"

He nodded.

"Tell me."

He shook his head.

"Come on."

"I don't know all your words for it."

"Tell me with your words," she said.

He hesitated. He hadn't recounted his histories for any human but Levi; he had been too embarrassed to let Charlotte record them, though now he wished he had agreed to it. He took a breath and haltingly began. She stared at him, and her eyes grew wide; one hand went up to her mouth, and he stopped.

"No, don't," she said.

"I don't want to," he said.

"Kato, you were singing. Mermaids sing!"

"Um...songs...they're easier to remember," he said.

"I know. Humans do it, too. People will come to see you sing," she said.

He shook his head. "No."

"Yes, people will come see it."

"Maybe."

She didn't press the issue after that. Later, Angel and Tad came, and the three of them peppered Kato with questions about what he could and couldn't do.

They decided on a series of physical things he could do, and he agreed to do it for real food.

"What do you mean real food?" Tad asked.

Kato held up the thing he had been eating for dinner. "Not real food."

"Fine, what do you want?" Angel asked.

"Sushi?" he asked.

"What the fuck do you mean sushi?" Angel asked.

"It's...like little fish with—"

"I know what sushi is. How do you know what sushi is?"

"Levi got it for me."

"Who the fuck is Levi?" One hand pinched the bridge of his nose.

"He's one of us, right?" Tess asked. "A human?"

Kato nodded. "My boyfriend."

They all turned to look at him.

"Your what?" Tad asked.

"Boyfriend."

"Like...*boyfriend* boyfriend?" Tess clarified.

"Uh..." Kato had no idea what she was trying to ask. "Yes?"

Angel laughed, for a long time, and Kato couldn't be sure why. He didn't ask because he didn't care. Finally, he said, "I'll see if I can get you some sushi, all right?"

Kato nodded.

For the weeks that followed, Kato practiced the obstacle course they had designed for him. Angel taught him how to throw a ball into a hoop with a net, and he managed to get it through about half the time. Tad taught him how to juggle, which he wasn't very good at and more often than not, he ended up tossing the balls away in frustration.

When he wasn't practicing, he floated. He stared up at the sky and looked at the clouds. He wondered what his friends were doing; he wondered if they were okay. He wondered, and it made his stomach hurt and his heart thrum to think about, if Levi had found someone else.

A day before his first appearance was slated, Tess called to him. "Hey."

He opened his eyes and looked at her. She held out a bag, and he swam over to take it; within he found an apple and a breakfast pastry.

"Morning," she said.

He ignored her while he ate.

"They'd kill us if they knew what we were feeding you."

He shoved the pastry into his mouth. It was too sweet and dry, but he ate it anyway because it was better than fish scraps. The apple he enjoyed more.

"You want to see something?"

He looked at her and saw she was holding out her phone, a video on the screen. He reached over and tapped the play button. Since he had tried to call for help, none of them had let him hold the phone, but sometimes they let him use it. Tad liked to show him videos of baby animals.

The scene he watched was jarringly alien until he realized it was a video of him, him and Levi on the day he had been captured. It killed his appetite to watch his own kidnapping, and he set aside the apple, grabbing onto Tess's wrist to hold the phone steadier.

"It went viral a few days ago," she said. "When they announced your name. You're real name. I guess when people Google you this is what comes up, too, not just the webpage for the park. Is that...that guy? Is he your boyfriend?"

Kato nodded. "Levi."

"They've been looking for you, I guess. I mean, everyone kind of figured...the people who saw it thought it was a fake. But it's getting a lot of views now."

He pressed the replay button for the video and watched it again and then a third time. He couldn't stop.

"We're supposed to go over your routine again today. Jim and Mike are coming by to watch."

Mike, he knew, was the man who always wore slacks, and Jim was another human in a skintight suit, but his had blue stripes instead of being all black. He had bitten both of them, and now they knew better than to come close. He made a face at the thought of them watching him.

"There's gonna be a lot of people here tomorrow," she said.

He shrugged.

"Are you nervous?"

"Which one is nervous?"

"It's...you know, if you're scared you're going to mess up."

"Oh. No. Not important."

She nodded.

Kato swished his tail in the water, holding a ball close to his chest, cradling it the way he'd hold a baby. He tried not to think of how long it had been since he'd held a child or heard a voice speak his own language. It hurt to breathe for a moment, and he squeezed his eyes shut until it passed.

"You know, um." Her voice pulled him back and he glanced at her. "I'm not from here either. I grew up, well, you don't know where it is, I bet, but we moved here when I was a teenager. I had friends there. And I haven't been back. I haven't seen my grandmother or my cousins."

He waited because her statement didn't feel finished.

"Just...I'd send you home if I could."

"Why...you have a job. Here."

"Yeah."

"For money?" he asked.

She nodded.

"Why?"

"'Cause I didn't think it was like this," she said. "And now, I'm just..." She shook her head. "I don't know."

He threw the ball away from him. Voices approached, and they looked up to see Tad, Angel, Mike and Jim walking toward them, all of them speaking in a lower tone, louder than normal. Their voices only changed like that when they were all together, and Kato didn't like it because they seemed to border on aggressive when in a group.

"Ready?" Angel asked.

Kato bared his teeth.

Mike made a face. "And you're trying to tell me he's a lot like us."

Angel rubbed the back of his neck. "He's...you know. He's upset."

Tess stood up.

"Come on," Angel said. "Last time before the big day."

Kato slunk into the water, giving Jim and Mike nasty looks the whole time. He half-assed his way through the show, and Tad said, "Come on, you're not gonna phone it in tomorrow, are you?"

Kato lunged for him; he yelped and jumped back. Kato laughed.

"He won't do that tomorrow," Jim said. "Will he?"

"No," the three assured him.

"'Cause you know, there's gonna be a reporter coming close to him."

"He won't. He knows to be good," Angel assured. "He just likes to pick on Tad."

"Everyone likes to pick on Tad," Tess said.

Kato retreated to his spot on the wall; he didn't want to listen to anything else they had to talk about. He didn't sleep well that night, and he blamed Tess for asking him if he was nervous.

In the morning, they came in and gave him breakfast, two oranges and a bag of cocktail shrimp; he saved one of the oranges for later, setting it on the ledge of the small pool where he slept most nights, except for when his skin bothered him; on those nights, he slept on the platform.

He heard voices talking, at first just a few, then dozens, then hundreds. His stomach twisted. He knew what he was supposed to do forward and backward; he could, and had, done it with his eyes closed. He didn't want to do it; he didn't want anyone to watch him. He swam over to the gate, and Angel said, "Hey, come on, you've got to wait until it starts."

He shook his head.

Angel knelt next to him. "It's gonna be okay, all right? They won't know if you mess up."

He reached out a hesitant hand and placed it on Kato's shoulder. Kato felt himself leaning into his hand, desperate for contact. In the sea, people were together all the time, sleeping in huddles, running their hands over other's arms and tails and brushing against each other as they swam.

"We'll be fine."

Kato nodded.

A few minutes later, in a perky voice that sounded nothing like her usual one, Tess said, "Now, today, I know I have a very special friend in the area, and I think if we can be very quiet he might come out."

The arena went silent, except for the wails of a few children. Kato waited for just a moment then pushed open the gate and slipped into the larger pool. He circled once to get his nerve up, and when he pulled himself up onto the platform next to Tess, the arena gasped collectively. He glanced up to see himself on a large screen.

Tess went through her script, a routine they'd practiced together, asking him to wave. He waved and people cheered. She asked him if he would sing, and he told a short history about Ta'lil the Impossible. People cheered again even though they hadn't understood a word he'd said.

They cheered when he did his stupid tricks and cheered more when he and Tad shot baskets together. They screamed when they were told they had been a great audience and were asked to come again.

They stayed and crowded close to the clear tank walls. Angel called him over to where a woman and man with a large camera waited. Kato knew what they were because he'd seen them in the movies.

The woman introduced herself to the camera, told them about Kato, what they'd just seen and then spoke with Angel, Tess and Tad for a while. Kato watched, twisting his hands together. When her turn was over, Tess whispered to him, "It's a live interview, anything you say everyone will see. They did the whole show live."

He nodded.

The reporter turned her attention to him once Tess had backed away, crouching down and saying, "Now, I've been told if I ask you what your name is, I might get a real surprise. They're not pulling my leg, are they?"

He shook his head.

"Well...I feel a little silly, but my name is Gwen," she said with a smile.

He looked at her for a moment, as frightened as he'd ever been, and said, "My name is Kato."

She gasped and laughed a little. "Oh, wow, I can't believe it." She looked at the camera then back at him. "Kato, is there anything you want to say? You just had a big day!"

He nodded. She spoke to him the way adults spoke to children, but he understood why. She thought he was stupid, or at least, stupider than her. Smart for an animal, maybe.

"I can say something?" he asked.

"Yeah, go ahead, I'm sure everyone watching would love to hear what you have to say. I still can't believe this!"

He glanced at the camera.

"You can talk to the camera," she said.

He looked into it and saw himself, distorted, looking back. "My name is Kato. I want to go home. Please help me."

Gwen stared at him, her mouth hanging open.

He said, "I want to go home, I don't want to be here. Please let me go home."

His throat tightened, and he knew his face was contorted, but he couldn't help it, he couldn't say anything else. He covered his face with his hands and couldn't help the keening sounds that slipped from his mouth.

From behind the camera, someone shouted for them to turn that shit off *immediately*, and the camera man fumbled in a hurry to obey. Gwen remained crouched next to them.

People started to shout, the reporter arguing with Mike and Jim, while they demanded to know from Tess, Angel, and Tad if they had known this would happen.

He slipped into the water while they fought and saw people were still pressed against the clear walls. A lot had left, discouraged by the sheer numbers. One little girl was raised up high above the others, sitting on her father's shoulders. Kato could have reached his hand over the wall and touched her.

He swam over, and people froze up, gasping and hissing to each other. He put two hands on the wall and pulled himself up.

"Hey!" he heard Angel call to him. "Kato!"

He reached out his hand to the little girl, propped up with one arm. She stared at him. Her father stared, too. She grabbed his hand, grinning.

"Kato, don't do that!" Angel called.

Kato ignored him. He was sure that Angel thought he would bite this girl like he bit the others, but he loved children, no matter if they were legged or not. "Hi," he said.

"Hi!"

An announcement rang out over the speakers, telling them that the exhibit was closed, that they had to leave so they could prepare for the next show.

"Did you like my song?" he asked the child.

She nodded. "You're like Ariel! She has hair, though."

He smiled, glad for the sound of a young voice, for the particular way children enunciated. "She does. Pretty hair like yours."

"Can you talk to fish?"

"Fish are very boring to talk to."

A man in uniform told the father they had to go. The girl looked heartbroken. Kato squeezed her hand and said, "That's okay. Don't be sad."

She held onto his hand for a moment then said, "I like your fingers."

He laughed.

She let go of his hand, and her father put her on the floor. Kato dove underwater and waved goodbye to her from there. She glanced back until they were out of the gate. When she was gone, he retreated to the smaller pool, rolling the orange he had set aside between his fingers. The humans yelled for a long time, at each other and in general, and he lay on his back with his ears underwater so he couldn't understand what they were saying.

They didn't do any more shows that day, though they had three more scheduled. No one came to check on him, not even Angel or Tess, who always said goodbye before they went home.

He waited for a long time for something to happen but nothing did. He heard far away voices, children shouting, faint voices over speakers, and the cries of animals, but no one else came to his exhibit. No one came to feed him, and he ate his orange, glad he had set it aside.

As it grew dark, he started to wonder if he had made the wrong choice. Tess didn't seem like she would get him in trouble on purpose. So far, the humans here had not done anything to hurt him, but when his fingers strayed to the scar Manit had left on his shoulder, he began to wonder what their punishments would be like.

The next morning, Tess didn't come in. Angel and Tad did. He grabbed Angel's hand and pointed to the tiny brunette who had come in with them.

"Tess got fired. She's the replacement."

Kato felt sick, and his hand flew to his throat.

"Fired?" he asked, thinking of the way Levi had thrown crabs onto the fire, thinking of the marshmallows they'd roasted, black and crispy. "Is...she..."

Angel crouched next to him. "I didn't think you and her were best pals. She took the blame for what you said yesterday so all of us wouldn't. I don't think she could have hacked it here much longer, anyway."

"She is dead?"

"What? No!"

"Fired," he said, "Fire is..." He rubbed his fingers together. "You cook things. It's hot."

"Shit, no," Angel said. "Fired just means you don't have your job anymore. She doesn't work here. She's not dead."

"Oh." Kato felt stupid and relieved.

"So cameras aren't allowed near you anymore, and you can't go near people."

"Or what?" Kato asked.

"I don't know," Angel admitted. "Your interview, what you said, it's going crazy on the Internet, though. They might shut the park down. I hear the president is going to do a press conference."

Kato smiled.

"And that other video? The one Tess found? I think...well, I don't know. Anyway, we have a show to do."

Kato nodded.

"And we're not allowed to bring you in food anymore."

Kato made a face.

"I'm sorry," he said.

Jim came by later in the morning and prowled about, looking at things, checking things that didn't need to be checked and harassing Angel. He didn't go near Kato because every time he took a step too close, Kato lunged for him.

They did all their scheduled shows for the day with the new girl in Tess's place. After each show, Kato swam over to the wall and propped himself up. He talked to the children and made them laugh. At the end of the day, when Mike came to yell at them, Angel explained that he didn't have a way to keep Kato from going over to them.

"Not anything that won't look like we're tying him up," he pointed out.

The next day they did four shows, and the day after. For three days, Kato went through his paces and talked to children. On the fourth day, they had guards rush the viewers out, to keep them away from the walls. Kato still tried to wave to them, and they would always wave back, calling his name. Jim came every morning and night to make sure things were in order and to make sure no food had been brought in.

On the sixth morning after his interview, as he picked through his bucket of scraps, he heard something more than just the normal chatter of the park.

He tugged on the leg of Tad's wetsuit, and Tad jumped then asked, "What?"

"What is?" he asked, waving one of his hands in the air to indicate the sound.

"The protesters?"

Kato shook his head.

"People came here. They're angry and they're...you know, chanting. They want the park to let you go."

"Will it work?"

"It didn't work for the whales," he said. "But whales can't talk."

"Everyone knows?"

"You mean, is it worldwide?"

Kato nodded, though he wasn't sure what worldwide really meant.

"Yeah. The Queen of England says it's deplorable, and the Pope says all God's creatures should be free," Tad said. "People want us to close the park."

"They're trying to say you can't go back," Angel told him. "Something about how you got washed up and hurt and you can't be on your own."

"I'm fine!" Kato insisted. "I swim all day."

Angel gestured to the scars on his tail. "Those are pretty gnarly."

Kato shook his head.

"Well, anyway, we've got a show."

Kato shrugged. He hated the shows, but they were a break from doing nothing. He liked making the children smile. He didn't like how at night sometimes he could hear the other captives, the keening of dolphins.

"Phone?"

"After," Angel said.

Kato nodded. He wasn't allowed to use phones, but Angel let him do it anyway. He made it through the day with phone access to look forward to, doing his act and then combing through everything he could find about himself on the Internet. So far he'd found out that his kidnapping video was wildly popular and his interview had gotten the reporter fired, but she'd been hired by another network and was working to help him. He hadn't found anything about his friends, nothing more than the pictures they had taken together and the video they had posted.

The protests continued and got louder. Every day he heard people chanting for his freedom. Two weeks went by, and Angel grew fidgety.

After their last show of the day, Kato touched his hand and asked, "What's wrong?"

He shook his head.

"Are they going to fired you, too?" He'd heard them fight about it.

"I don't know." He sat down next to Kato and handed over his phone. Kato took it but just held it.

Angel said after a quiet minute, "They're gonna try something."

"Who?"

"The park owners. They're gonna try to move you. Get you somewhere where they wouldn't care if you're a person or not."

Kato's grip tightened on the phone.

"They think I'm on board," he said. "But...you know...shit, this is bad enough."

Kato nodded.

"I don't know when. I don't know how this is going to turn out. I want to tell you I won't let it happen, but there's probably not much I can do."

"Will you help me find my friends?" he asked. "If they...I want to see them. If they want to see me."

"The people in the video, right? I'll, uh, I'll look into. See if I can get a hold of them through their website."

Kato nodded. "Website?"

"Yeah." Angel took his phone back, pulled up a site, then handed it over.

Kato looked at it then said, "Too many words. I can't read it."

"They've been looking for you. They've got a lot of hotshots in Hollywood on board and some lawyer from New York. They didn't forget about you if that's what you're worried about."

Kato shrugged, and Angel patted him on the back. They did their shows; Kato pulled himself through them, distracted and making mistakes. People cheered anyway. He stomached a little bit of his dinner then retreated to the smaller pool.

The next morning, Angel came in and found him lying on the platform. He had been there all night, unable to sleep but not motivated to do anything else.

Angel sat beside him, his legs crossed like a pretzel, and asked, "Are you okay?"

Kato opened his eyes, looked over then shook his head. Angel sighed and eyed him critically.

"How long have you been up here?"

He shook his head. "Don't know."

"Shouldn't you be in the water?"

"Doesn't matter."

"I don't know. You look...grayer than you usually do. And kind of sticky." He reached out a hand and touched Kato's arm. "Yeah, you're sticky. Is it normal?"

"Happens sometimes."

"Well, is it a bad thing? Are you sick? I really think you should get in the water."

Kato shook his head. "The water, it's not right. It makes...um..." He scratched at his arm.

"Itchy?"

"Yeah."

"That's probably the chlorine. How are your eyes doing?" he asked, peering at Kato's face.

"They hurt."

Angel sighed and rubbed his face. "If I call a vet, will you bite them?"

"Yes," he said because he had bitten almost everyone who had come near him, except for Tess and Angel.

"I might have to do it anyway." He reached out and touched Kato's skin again. "You're warm."

"Happens sometimes."

Angel pinched his skin.

"Ouch!"

"You're dehydrated." He handed Kato his phone and said, "Don't get it wet." Then he walked away.

Kato rolled onto his stomach and tapped in his name like he did whenever he had access to the Internet. There were no new videos or pictures about him. He wondered if he should do something to get people's attention. After he checked for news, he Googled dog, which was one of the words the iPad had taught him to spell and spent some time looking at pictures of dogs.

Angel returned and said, "Hey, eat this."

Kato glanced up and saw him holding a tray of yellowish clear cubes. "What is it?"

"Jello."

He sat up, eager.

"Who the fuck fed you Jello?" Angel asked, "Are you some kind of garbage disposal?" He sat back down and balanced the tray on his lap.

Kato didn't answer, grabbed a cube and looked at it more closely. "What flavor?"

"Fucking...plain."

"Plain?"

"Just eat it before I have to use the hose on you," Angel said.

Kato frowned, not sure what it would entail but not liking the way Angel had said it. He ate the cube and found it tasteless.

"I like cherry."

"We don't have cherry. We have plain."

"And grape."

"I'm not allowed to give you anything else," he said.

"Why not?"

"'Cause they're afraid I might make you sick," he said.

Kato snorted.

"What?"

He shook his head and took another cube. It tasted like nothing, which was better than the old fish taste from the scraps he usually ate. "I like Dori-toes."

Angel laughed. "Dor-ee-toes."

"Dori-toes. That's what I said."

"I don't have Doritos, and I can't give them to you."

"You can't give me the phone either but you do."

"They check me for food now when I come in, and they check me after lunch."

"I like juice. And spaghetti. Both sauces. Red and white. And...um. Little round candies? Lots of colors?"

"Chocolate or fruit?"

"Fruit."

"Skittles."

"I like Skittles."

"Do you trust me?" Angel asked.

"What?"

"Do you trust me?"

"Why?" he asked, narrowing his eyes.

"Yes or no?"

"I don't know," Kato said.

"I'm going to need you to," he said. "Eat the rest of those. And your breakfast."

Kato made a face, but he ate some of it.

He meandered through his shows for the week and had Jello with his breakfast and dinner every morning. He pulled Mike into the water and held him under for a half a minute and bit Jim hard on the arm, enough to make him bleed and come in the next day with a bandage wrapped around his arm.

In the middle of the night, Kato heard voices and noises. He sat up and edged close to the pool, nervous. He was more than nervous; he was scared.

"Kato?" he heard Angel call softly. "It's just me. I can't turn the lights on. Can you come over to me? I'm on the stairs."

He thought very much about sliding into the water and hiding there, but he thought about what Angel had asked him, about if he trusted him. He pulled himself over to the stairs and under the full moon he could see Angel was not alone, four other people accompanied him. In the light of the moon and stars, and with the handful of lights on at night, he could make out who they were.

One of them was a guard Kato often saw wandering around at night. They waved to each other usually. The other three he recognized after a moment and clapped his hands to his mouth.

"You need to stay quiet," the guard warned.

Kato wasn't listening. Levi had pushed past the guard and Angel and knelt next to him. Kato grabbed him and buried his face in his shirt, pressing against him as hard as he could. After a moment, Levi took Kato's face in his hands and said, "Let me look at you for a second."

Kato sniffled and rubbed a few tears off his face with the back of his hand.

"What happened to you? You look like shit," Levi said. "What's wrong with your eyes? Why are you all sticky!"

"Levi!" he heard Emily hiss. "That's *not nice.*"

"What do you mean, sticky?" Charlotte asked.

Levi had crushed him to his chest again and even though it was uncomfortable, Kato wouldn't have traded it for anything.

The girls came over, and he hugged them, too, even Charlotte who pulled back after a moment and said, "Ugh, you are sticky!"

"Shh," the guard reminded.

Angel said, "Uh, the park wouldn't let them in during the day, 'cause of, you know, the bad press. I probably...you know, it's like a one-time thing."

Kato looked at him.

"Listen, I'm sorry, but we can't sneak people in every night. And I can't get you out."

Kato shook his head and looked worriedly at Levi then Emily. "Don't leave me here."

"I'm not," Levi said immediately. "I won't. I promise."

"Levi," Emily tried to gently gain his attention.

"Em, I can't leave him!" Levi cried, distraught.

"Levi, we have a plan," Charlotte reminded him. "A good plan."

"What plan?" Kato asked.

Angel said, "They're moving you south of the border in a couple days."

"But we're not going to let them," Emily assured. "Angel is going to go with you, let us know what way they're taking you, and we'll do something to block off the road. We promise. It'll be better that way. We can't get you out past all the other guards. It was hard enough sneaking in."

She held his hand as she said it, and he felt better.

"So just a couple more days, okay?" she said.

He nodded.

"What's he doing with his tail?" Angel glanced at the way he had twined himself around Levi's legs and settled into his lap. "Is that a...you know, a gay thing?"

Emily glanced up and giggled, then to a cross-looking Charlotte said, "Shhhh, not now, okay. He's helping us out."

Charlotte crossed her arms.

Levi cradled him close. "Have you been okay?"

He shook his head. "No."

"You're really warm."

"Doesn't matter."

"I'm sorry about all of this."

"You didn't do anything."

Levi hugged him tighter.

"Not your fault," Kato assured. "I miss you."

"I missed you, too. A lot."

"Your classes...they are good?"

Levi sniffled. "I haven't been going, I couldn't. With you...God, we didn't know what had happened to you, and I was so worried."

"Oh."

Levi hugged him tighter. "Are you okay? Why are you so warm? Why are you sticky?"

"Happens sometimes," Kato said.

"But *why?*" Levi asked. "Are you sick?"

"I will be better," he said. "Good water, good food. I will get better."

He tried not to think about the itchy, tender patches all over his body or the constant pain in his stomach and head; he didn't think about how his eyes burned or the way some of his teeth had grown loose in his gums. Once he was home, he would be better, he knew; all he needed was clean water and real food.

"You promise?" Levi asked.

"Yes," he said. "It happens sometimes. With bad water."

He was not a child, and he was not very old; this would probably not kill him, and if it did, it would take a long time. He hoped it would not take a long time to get home.

Levi squeezed him.

"Do you guys want a minute?" Emily asked.

Kato nodded, and she took Charlotte's hand, the two of them walking away and taking the guard and Angel with them. Once they'd gotten to the bottom of the stairs, Kato ran his fingers over Levi's face. "Still byouiful."

"So are you."

"Even though I am sticky?"

Levi's face scrunched up, and he nodded. Kato kissed him, just for a moment; he had not thought about kissing or sex in a long time. The world had felt too dark and barren to think about those sorts of things, but now Levi was here and things were brighter.

"You still love me, yes?" he asked. "There isn't anyone else?"

"What? No, of course not." Levi wiped his eyes and after a moment said, "Kato, I never said it, that I loved you. I should have. I'm sorry. It's just, I thought we had more time."

Kato shook his head, confused. "Why would you say it?"

"So you would know I did," Levi said.

"No. Love isn't something you say. It's something you do. Humans really do that? Like in the movies?"

"Yes."

Kato snorted. "Stupid."

"I know."

He rested his head against Levi's chest and listened to him breathe for a few minutes. "How is your family?"

"Uh. Weird. Well, I mean...yeah, weird."

"Why weird?"

"Because they know about you now," he said.

"Oh."

"But I don't care."

"They are mad at you?"

"It's just...it's really weird right now, and I don't know how things are going to work out," Levi said.

Kato sighed. "I want to go home."

Levi's arms tightened around him and a sob slipped out. "I know, I want you home too."

"What's wrong?"

"It's not...you know. I don't know if it would be safe for you. Someone already took you once, and now they'll know, people will know where you are." He choked.

Kato pulled back. "Then where?"

"I don't know."

Kato shook his head, feeling cold and sick. He had nowhere else to go; his family had exiled him and going back would mean death just as much as trying to survive the open ocean alone would. He needed somewhere safe and sheltered to go at night; he needed friends to talk to and someone to love. Going back to the sea would be no better than being here; he would still be alone, and he would still die.

"Can't," he said.

"Don't...Kato, don't cry, it's just...we don't know what we're going to do. But I know we're going to get you out of here first. Okay? I promise."

Kato sniffed and nodded.

"Hey, uh," the guard called. "My shift is over soon. We gotta head out."

Kato squeezed him with everything he had, and Levi squeezed him back. The girls came back over, and he hugged Emily, too. She cried, and he promised her things would be okay.

Charlotte regarded him for a moment, gave him a quick hug and said, "When you're out, I want to show you want I found about those markings."

He stared for a moment, having forgotten entirely about the pictures he had taken for her, and then said, "Okay."

"It'll be important, you know, to show how you're real people, that you're like us. From a legal standpoint."

He nodded, not sure what she meant and having no idea how he could prove he was a real person. He watched them go, and they all promised they would see each other soon. Kato wanted to believe it; he couldn't really, but he tried.

Late the following afternoon, after his last show, he saw the guard from the night before shooing people out of the arena; he slipped into the water and went over, pulling himself up and leaning over the edge.

"Hey," he called.

The man looked over then shook his head. "You're not supposed to do that."

"I didn't remember to say thank you," Kato said.

"You don't have to."

"It was good."

"Yeah, well," the man glanced around. "You know, it was always a little weird working here," he confessed in a soft voice. "You know, they did the same thing to black folk back in the day, put 'em on display. Hearing you talk, seeing you in a tank...it just doesn't sit right."

"Black?"

"Sure, like me."

"And Angel?"

"Nah, not Angel. He's Mexican," the guard said.

Kato shrugged. "Not important. Thank you."

The man nodded then glanced around and walked over to a couple who had lingered, trying to take pictures.

Kato retreated back to his platform and said to Tad, "Phone."

"I'm not supposed to."

He put out his hand and waited. Tad sighed and retrieved his phone, handing it over nervously.

"You're going to get me in trouble."

Kato bared his teeth, just a little; it was half-hearted.

The new girl, whose name Kato still didn't know, said, "You're not supposed to do that. You're not even supposed to have your phone back here."

"It's not really a big deal," Tad said.

The girl gave Kato a nasty look, which took him by surprise. He looked up at Tad and asked, "What's wrong with her?"

"She likes to follow the rules," Tad said.

"Yeah, well, she can go get some Jello," Angel said with a pointed glance.

The girl looked over then walked away.

"Come here," Angel said.

"Why?"

"I need to take some pictures of you," he said.

Kato frowned then pulled himself over to where Angel was. "For what?"

"Show me those spots you were talking about before, the ones that hurt," he said.

"Why?"

"Because you said you'd bite the vet," Angel said. "And I'm worried about them."

"I'm going home soon," Kato said. "I'll be better there."

"It'll just make me feel better," he said.

Kato huffed but allowed Angel to document all his ailments, down to his loose teeth and his irritated eyes.

"How are you feeling?" Angel asked.

Kato stared at his phone and sat up a little straighter.

"Are you doing a movie?" he asked.

"No, that would be stupid, Kato," Angel said pointedly, and Kato frowned, not sure what his tone meant but knowing it wasn't good. "Tell me how you're feeling."

"I want to go home. I feel...wrong. All the time. I'm tired, and I can't sleep, and I'm bored. I hate this."

Angel tapped his phone, and it booped. Kato grabbed his hand, and Angel said,

Don't worry about it."

Angel patted his back, and when the girl returned, said, "Make sure you eat those."

Kato nodded and ate one. It tasted of nothing, but at this point, even the fish tasted like nothing. He couldn't remember what food or water was supposed to taste like anymore.

"Angel?" he asked.

Angel looked over. "What?"

"I can hear them sometimes," he said. "The others here. I'm not the only exhibit."

He said it slowly, hoping to be told he was wrong, that the wails of dolphins were pumped over the speaker just to make him miserable.

"Yeah."

"Will anyone help them?"

"You will," Angel said. "Now stop talking and eat before we get in trouble."

He ate a few more cubes and some fish. He wondered if his friends would really make him find somewhere else to live; maybe their beach was not as safe as they had thought, but it was the only place he had to go back to. He wondered if Levi would ever bring him dinner again or if Emily would ever show him a drawing she'd done of him; he wondered if he would ever listen for hours as Charlotte explained something.

"That's not enough, you have to eat more," Angel said.

He looked up.

"If he's not eating, you should—" the girl began.

"It's my call if he needs it or not," Angel snapped.

She gave him a dirty look and walked away.

"I'll see you in the morning," Angel said. "Make sure you eat the rest. Please."

Kato nodded. He ate as much as he could then spent another night sleeping fitfully.

A week later, when his shows were done and everyone had gone home, Angel came with a lot of men he didn't recognize, as well as Mike and Jim. Jim had a pink, mouth-shaped scar on his forearm, and Kato felt grimly proud of the mark.

The strangers carried a sling, and one of the strangers he recognized as the vet. The vet carried a bag, and Kato eyed it suspiciously, recalling the prodding he'd endured before.

"Get him ready, we've got a schedule," Mike said.

The vet set down his bag and bent over it for several minutes. He stood with a needle in hand, and Kato immediately slunk closer to the water. He had not yet slid half his body into the water when he felt half a dozen hands on his tail, grabbing hard and pulling back, wrenching his muscles in the wrong direction.

He heard Angel protest, but the men held him down, their knees on his chest. He writhed and thrashed; the vet watched from a safe distance with Mike and Jim.

"Let me do it," Angel said.

Kato looked at him.

"You'll let me do it, right?" Angel asked, needle in hand. "Remember what we talked about?"

"What did you talk about?" Mike asked.

"That we're friends," Angel lied. He had never once called them friends, but he trained his green eyes on Kato's face.

Kato nodded. "Friends."

"Let him up. You're gonna really hurt him one of these days," Angel said.

The men looked at Mike, who asked Angel, "You've got this?"

"Sure."

Mike nodded, and the men stepped back but not too far. Angel knelt behind him and said, "It's just going to put you to sleep for a little while."

Kato watched as he brought the needle around to a more hidden spot and squirted the liquid within onto the floor before he jabbed it into his tail. Kato flinched and frowned then rubbed the spot when Angel pulled away.

"Just take it easy. It'll put you out soon," he assured.

Kato crossed his arms then lay down to look at the sky. He closed his eyes and waited for nothing to happen. He pretended to be asleep and had to keep himself from flinching when strange hands lifted him then carried him away in the sling. He peeked an eye open once and saw he was not in his exhibit anymore.

He snapped his eye shut and thought of the times as a child he had pretended to be asleep so his parents would carry him. He wondered if they worried about him or if they had forgotten him; they had other children, better-behaved ones, and grandchildren to care about. He wondered if they would be upset with him for getting caught, for making friends with the things that poisoned and dirtied their home.

He wondered for the first time if Levi was right to worry about what their families would think about them being together. He had no family to go to, but Levi still had parents he should be with.

The men loaded him into a truck, depositing him unceremoniously onto a hard, cold floor. He flinched from the coldness, not meaning to, but no one said anything. He was secured with rough ties that dug into the tender patches on his skin. The door was closed with a loud crash.

After a while, they moved. He opened his eyes to find it still very dark. The movement jostled him, and he tried to arrange himself more comfortably. He would be home after this; at least, he hoped so. It was what Emily had described. The only thing that could go wrong would be if Angel had lied.

But if Angel had been lying, he would have given him the shot the right way, and he wouldn't have snuck his friends in.

Kato didn't know how long went by, but he grew hungry and thirsty; he hadn't had anything to eat since lunch and hated how he found himself thinking first of the fish parts they fed him instead of real food. He flexed his hands and wondered if he would still be clever enough to catch a fish on his own.

The truck slammed to a stop, screeching and sliding, and the ties holding him bit hard into him, scraping against his skin. A buckle jabbed into his ribs.

The door opened a moment later, and Angel rushed in, his fingers working at the buckles. Kato touched blood smeared across the human's mouth, and Angel brushed his hand away.

"It's fine, I just had to deal with the driver."

Angel picked him up, and Kato clung to him. Outside of the truck, the sky was dark but the road was lit up so bright it hurt his eyes. He pressed his face against Angel's chest for a moment then looked up and saw that not just one or two cars blocking the road, but that dozens were, their head lights on full blast. The cars were all empty and maybe a hundred people had crowded around.

He saw Tess and waved to her. She waved back and opened the door to a car parked on the side of the road. Emily was behind the wheel of her Jeep with Levi in the back. Angel slid him into the backseat. He gripped Kato by the forearm for a moment. "Hey, don't get caught again."

"You get fired?"

"I guess I fucking quit," Angel said, a grim set about his mouth. "Get out of here."

Kato nodded. Angel stepped back and closed the door, checking to make sure Kato's tail wasn't hanging out. He and Tess watched, waving, as they pulled away. Emily maneuvered the Jeep back onto the road, and other people flocked to their cars, pulling out of the way. Levi wrapped his arms around him and pulled him close. Kato winced when his arms tightened around the place where the buckle had dug into him.

"What's wrong?"

Kato touched the sore spot. "Just hurts here."

"You look terrible," he said, "You're so skinny."

"Levi!" Emily scolded from the front seat.

"Have you been eating? Did they feed you? You're sick. I know you are, Kato, don't shake your head. What did they—"

Kato kissed him because he couldn't remember which of their many weird sounds was meant to tell someone to be quiet. He remembered after a moment and pulled away.

"Shh. I'm home."

"Not yet," Emily said, but it sounded more like she was saying it to herself than to him.

"Where's Charlotte?"

"She's waiting at home with my parents. She didn't, um, you know, she gets worked up."

"Your parents?" he asked.

"Sure, defending the civil rights of mermaids is the hottest new trend in Hollywood. They've got a news crew waiting and everything."

Kato shook his head.

"They think publicity is the best way to go with this," Levi explained. "You've got a lawyer and a PR person."

"What?"

"Lawyers work with the law, the rules. We're trying to make it so this can't happen again," Levi said. "And PR people, well, they make sure everything looks good, that people see what they want to see."

"Like porn."

"Exactly," Levi said. "You should try to get some sleep. We've got a little while before we're home."

Kato nodded and nestled as close as he could.

Kato woke up when the Jeep stopped. He looked up, trying to see the house or the beach, but all he saw were red and blue lights so bright he had to close his eyes. Levi was holding on to him too hard again, and Emily was swearing to herself.

A woman in uniform came up and peered into the window Emily had rolled down. She asked, "Do you know how fast you were going?"

"I'm sorry," Emily said immediately.

The officer peered into the backseat, frowned, took out a flashlight then shone it on them. She kept frowning.

"Ma'am, what is in your backseat?"

"Just my friends," Emily said, her voice shaking.

"I'm gonna have to ask you to open the back door of your car."

"For speeding? They weren't driving. Why do they need to get out?"

"Ma'am, what is that thing in your backseat?"

Kato sat up, and Levi wouldn't let him move. Kato pushed his hands away and leaned over to the window, pushing the button to roll it down. The woman stared.

"My name is Kato. I'm trying to go home," he said.

"You're the thing from the park. The mermaid."

He nodded. "I'm trying to go home. Will you let me go home?" he asked.

He was not sure of the exact function of police in the human world, but he knew they had authority and feared this woman could get him brought back to where he had been, returned to Mike and Jim.

"Please."

She looked at him for a long time and then took a step back.

"Get out of here," she said to Emily. "Watch your speed. I don't know about the other guys out tonight."

"Thank you." Emily's voice came out small and nervous.

Kato said, "Thank you."

"Yeah, well, my daughter's crazy about you. Couldn't go home and tell her I sent you back there," the officer said.

He rolled up the window, she walked away, and Emily started to drive again, this time not as fast.

Kato lay back down and couldn't fall back asleep. He played with Levi's fingers and asked, "Your parents are there, too?"

"No, just Emily's."

"Oh."

Levi sighed. "Maybe...you know, once we get settled back in. I could see, if you wanted, if they'd come out."

"Maybe."

He dozed through the rest of the ride, and when they got home, Levi got out of the car then pulled Kato into his arms and brought him down to the beach. Kato looked back and saw that someone was filming in. He squinted and saw the woman talking was the same reporter who had lost her job over his first interview.

He waved to her. She waved back and said something inaudible to the camera.

Levi carried him into the water, and Kato said, "Your shoes!"

"It's fine, they'll dry off," Levi said.

Levi waded in chest deep and loosened his arms. Kato still held on to him, though he relished the feel of good, clean water on his skin. He sank in up to his eyes and let the ocean hold him for a minute. He didn't let go of Levi's hand.

"Do you feel better?" Levi asked.

He nodded. He did a little bit. The salt stung his skin, but it was a clean, antiseptic sting. He circled once around Levi and tugged at his shorts then wrapped himself back around him.

"Am I supposed to leave?" Kato asked.

"You can."

"Do I have to?"

"No."

"Do you want me to?"

"No!"

"I stay, then."

"Don't, though, just because of me."

"It is more than because of you," he said. "Emily and Charlotte, they are here, too. And...I want to make sure this won't happen to another person like me. And the other things won't be there, the...uh...whiles?"

"Whales."

"They shouldn't be there either."

"I know."

Kato looked up at the beach and saw the camera crew had come down.

"Are they going to watch us all the time?"

"No."

"Good," he said. "I'm hungry."

"What do you want?" Levi asked.

"I need fish. To catch it. By myself."

Levi nodded.

"I need to swim." He couldn't make himself let go of Levi's hand.

"Sure."

He tightened his grip on Levi's fingers. "Just a little while."

"I understand."

"But come back," Kato said. "Make sure you come back."

"I will."

Kato reached up and wrapped his arms around his neck. "And bring me Skittles when you come back."

Levi smiled.

Kato kissed him. "Just a little while."

"You told me already," Levi said, only managing to be half-playful.

Kato made himself let go and slipped into the water, all the way, and swam off, jumpy and overly careful, but glad to be back where he belonged.

By the time Levi returned, Kato had given himself a stomachache scarfing down anything he could get his hands on. He shook his head at the Skittles when Levi offered them.

"Ate too much."

Levi laughed. "They want to talk to you."

"Who?"

"Everyone."

"Now?" he asked, a knot starting in his stomach.

"I can tell them you're not ready."

"No...I...uh," Kato said, looking around. "I can do it."

"You don't have to," Levi said gently.

"You stay with me?"

"Sure."

"I can do it now."

"Okay," Levi said and waved to the reporter.

She came down to meet them at the water's edge and smiled when she saw Kato. "Hi, I don't know if you remember me."

He nodded. "Gwen."

She smiled wider. "Yeah. I won't take long, okay?"

"Levi will stay with me." Kato took Levi's hand again and slithered his tail closer to Levi's legs. He would wrap him up and never let go as soon as he had the chance.

"That's fine. People are wild about you two," she said.

Kato glanced at Levi, and he said, "She means they think it's hilarious the only mermaid we've ever found is gay."

"What is gay?" Kato asked. "Everyone says it."

"It just means you're a boy who likes boys," Levi said.

"Oh."

"So are you ready?" Gwen asked.

Kato nodded and tightened his grip on Levi's hand. The first time he'd looked into a camera, it had been nothing, but after hours of scrolling through news sites, he had a deeper understanding of what was going to happen. People would see this, not just a few, but thousands, maybe even millions, which was more humans than Kato could fathom. They would fight about it, put videos of their arguments on the Internet, and turn out in droves to chant for his freedom.

She and the cameraman bustled around for a few minutes, getting them to sit right and make sure everything looked the way it was supposed to, or at least, as Kato understood it, the way people expected things to look.

Finally, she asked him to share what had happened to him.

He had not expected the question, and he definitely hadn't expected it to be first. He knew his face had gone slack, and he made himself take a breath. Levi put his other hand on his forearm.

Kato asked, "Do you want to know everything or just what happened...um." He thought and whistled to himself when he couldn't find the world. "Not a long time before, just..."

"Right before?"

He nodded. "Do you want to know what happened right before?"

"Why don't you tell us everything?" she asked.

"It's not...short sort—story. It is longer."

"That's fine. People want to know."

He took a breath and told what had happened from the day Emily had found him in the pickup truck until his very recent rescue. Halfway through, he started to cry, and the woman offered him a tissue, which he took but didn't know what to do with.

"It's for your face," Levi whispered.

"Why?"

"So it won't be wet."

Kato couldn't help but laugh, and Levi laughed, too. It was easier to finish his story, the tissue still clutched in his hand, unused.

After that, the woman and the cameraman left him alone.

To Levi, he said, "I'm sleepy."

"Do you want me to go so you can sleep?"

"No," he said with a firm shake of his head. "I want you to take me to your bed."

"You'll be all right?"

"Yes."

"Okay," Levi said.

Kato wrapped his arm around his neck, and Levi lifted him like he was nothing. He knew he should hold on tighter or try to support himself to some degree, but he had no strength left. Levi brushed most of the sand off Kato and himself and kept his eyes on the floor as they walked past Emily and her parents.

Charlotte waved, and Kato waved back.

"Tomorrow we'll talk," she said, and he nodded. It was all he could manage.

Levi set him down on the bed and said, "Uh."

"What?"

"I have to brush my teeth."

"Okay."

"I'll be right back." He ducked out of the room, seeming uncomfortable.

Kato didn't take it personally.

When Levi came back, he got into bed next to Kato, and his mouth didn't taste like his mouth but like something else. It was sweet and strong, and Kato almost didn't mind the smell.

He ran his fingers over Levi's face for a little while.

"What are you doing?" Levi asked.

"Nothing."

"I thought you were tired."

"I am."

"So go to sleep."

"Do you want me to say that thing? Like in the movies?"

"What? I love you?"

"Yes."

"No. If you wouldn't say it normally, don't say it now," Levi said.

"But...if you were me, you would say it?"

"Do you mean if you were some stupid human with stupid legs?"

"Yes."

"You still might not say it," Levi said.

"Stupid," Kato said.

"I know."

Kato burrowed as deep into the bed as he could, twining himself around Levi and getting lost in the covers.

"Tomorrow, I show you love," Kato promised.

"Yeah?"

"Yeah. And then we save the whales."

"Sounds totally reasonable and achievable."

Into Levi's chest, in a series of clicks and whistles, he expressed his disdain for humanity and their horrible, incomprehensible words.

Levi kissed his head and said, "Stop badmouthing me and go to sleep."